DANNY ORLIS
AND THE
GUATEMALA ADVENTURE

DANNY ORLIS

AND THE

GUATEMALA ADVENTURE

BERNARD PALMER

Please note that several books in the Danny Orlis series are published by Sword of the Lord Publications and are available for purchase on their website, www.swordbooks.com.

Danny Orlis and the Guatemala Adventure
© 2024 by Bernard Palmer
All rights reserved. First edition 1968.
Second edition 2024.

Scripture quotations from The Authorized (King James) Version. Rights in the Authorized Version in the United Kingdom are vested in the Crown. Reproduced by permission of the Crown's patentee, Cambridge University Press.

Cover image: Adobe Firefly
Character illustrations: John Ball
Editor: Charlene Miskimen

Aneko Press Youth

www.anekopress.com

Aneko Press, Life Sentence Publishing, and our logos are trademarks of Life Sentence Publishing, Inc.
203 E. Birch Street
P.O. Box 652
Abbotsford, WI 54405

JUVENILE FICTION / Religious / Christian / Action & Adventure

Paperback ISBN: 979-8-88936-040-7
eBook ISBN: 979-8-88936-041-4
10 9 8 7 6 5 4 3 2 1
Available where books are sold

CONTENTS

CHAPTER 1

BACK TO GUATEMALA

It was almost morning, and the vast city was still slumbering when the Minneapolis bus pulled into the Chicago station. Danny Orlis sat up and looked around. For a time sleep blurred his vision and numbed his mind. The lights in the bus came on, and he shook himself awake.

"Kay." He reached over and touched his young wife on the shoulder. "Kay, we're in Chicago."

"Oh." She jerked upright. "I didn't realize how tired I was. I must have fallen asleep shortly after we left our last stop."

They got up and made their way out of the bus.

"I think we'd better stay here in the city tonight. We can go out to Wheaton in the morning."

"It doesn't seem possible that we're on our way back to Guatemala after we've been away so long."

"We're only going to be there a few weeks," he reminded her.

"I know." A wistful tone crept back into her voice. "But maybe we'll be there long enough to find out that I'll be able to stand the climate now."

Danny did not answer her. This was one of the things he had been afraid of when he had been asked to fly the new mission airplane down to Guatemala and test it under field conditions. Nobody missed a mission field any more than Kay missed being in Guatemala. It had been the big despair of her life.

At first, he hadn't even thought about taking Kay along to Guatemala while he tested the new type of plane. They probably wouldn't have thought about it if they hadn't been invited to dinner with Pastor and Mrs. Reeves that evening.

"I don't mind telling you, Danny," the minister said when they finished eating and were sitting in the living room, "I'm fascinated by the new plane you're testing. It sounds as though it's going to be a tremendous help to missionaries."

"I think it's going to be a tremendous thing. It's got capacity to haul big loads, and with two engines, there's an added margin of safety that's been needed for a long time."

"How long will you be gone?"

Danny shrugged his shoulders. That was a question he had been asking himself. It would have to be flown under varying conditions with actual workloads. The logical way would be to use it to service mission stations as though it were permanently stationed there.

"Maybe four or five weeks. Maybe a couple of months or more, according to the way the plane performs."

"Where's Jim Morgan going to stay while you're gone?" Mrs. Reeves put in.

"Jim? With Kay, of course."

Both the pastor and his wife looked quickly at Kay.

"Aren't you going with Danny to Guatemala?"

She shook her head. "We couldn't leave Jim alone."

"That's one of the reasons we asked you over tonight. We wanted to invite him to stay with us while you're gone."

At first Danny and Kay protested that it was an imposition on them, but when they insisted, they decided to take advantage of the opportunity.

Now they had completed the first leg of their journey.

Danny spent the next several days familiarizing himself with the new aircraft. He went over it carefully with the builders, learning all he could about the plane. Then he was checked out in it and flew it several more days so he could handle it as well as he handled the 180. Only then did he feel competent to take the new aircraft across country.

The day before they were to leave Wheaton, a missionary couple from Guatemala was speaking in one of the local churches. Danny and Kay went to hear them and waited afterward to talk with them. They were both very interested in the plane Danny was flying down to the field to test and asked a host of questions about it. At last all of their questions were answered.

"What is it like in Guatemala now?" Kay asked. She tried to sound casual, but her voice was taut.

"There have been a good many changes," the missionary said, "just as there have been a lot of changes everywhere. But our area is about the same as it was when we first went there fifteen years ago. The people seem to be just as poor and needy as they've ever been."

"Where will you be going first?" his wife asked.

Kay frowned. "I'm sorry, but I don't remember the name of the place. All I can think of now is that we're going to be staying with some missionaries by the name of Davis."

The other woman's eyes widened. "I'm sure you'll find that interesting."

Her husband chuckled. "You can say that again. In fact, I'd go so far as to suggest that you'll find it a memorable experience."

* * *

The following morning Danny and Kay got up before daylight. The sky was dark with foreboding, but it had not snowed for several hours, and the ceiling was at least eight hundred to one thousand feet. Neither of them spoke until they had transferred their luggage to the aircraft and Danny was warming up the engines. Kay fastened her seat belt and waited, sitting with her eyes closed.

"And what are you dreaming about, Kay?"

She straightened and faced him. "I was just sitting here thinking about that terrible day when we had to leave Guatemala a few years ago. I was sure then that we would never get a chance to go back, not even for a visit. But now we're on our way! I've been so happy and excited about it that I haven't been able to sleep nights."

Danny checked the gauges carefully and began to taxi to the end of the runway in preparation for takeoff.

"Danny, do you think we'll be able to go back to our old station while we're in Guatemala?"

"I hope so. If things work out so we can, I'd like to go over there and stay for a few days."

"That would be wonderful!" There was a new note in her voice – a sort of desperate longing – mingling with the joy. "Do you think they'll remember us? The people, I mean."

"Oh, sure. We have some wonderful Christian friends at the station. I'm positive they'll remember us."

There was a brief silence. When Kay spoke her voice was wooden and far away, as though she was not actually herself. It was as though she was suddenly transported to that land she loved so much. "You don't know how many times I've thought about the Indian people we used to work with in Guatemala," she said. "I've wondered so often how they have gotten along spiritually and which ones remained true."

He revved the engines and, satisfied that all was in order, started down the runway, quickly gathering speed.

They flew to Mexico City that day and stayed with missionary friends. The following morning they went on to Guatemala City where Tom and Phyllis Fowler, the missionaries stationed in the capital, met them at the airport.

"We're so glad you planned your trip so you can spend the night with us," Phyllis said. "It's been so long since we've seen you that we've got a lot to talk about."

Danny nodded. "We wouldn't miss a chance to visit with you."

Later that evening, when they had finished dinner and were about ready to go to bed, Kay asked the Fowlers to come down and visit them while they were living in Guatemala.

"That would be nice," Tom Fowler agreed. "It's been a long time since we've taken any time off. Where are you going to be based, Danny?"

"We would have liked to go back to our old station and use that as headquarters, but the board felt it wasn't centrally located. They suggested we stay with the Davises."

Phyllis Fowler gasped. "You're going to be at Cielo?" she echoed. "With Jerry and Rosalita Davis?"

Danny caught the inflection in her voice. "That's right, but now you've got me curious. Just what's the matter with them?"

"Nothing. Nothing at all. In fact they are two of our best missionaries. They're doing a tremendous piece of work."

Danny still was not satisfied. "That may be," he retorted, "but why is it that everywhere we go people laugh when they learn that we're going to be staying with them. What's the deal, anyway?"

Tom glanced at his wife. "Should we tell them?"

Phyllis's eyes were dancing. "I think it's much better if they find it out for themselves."

"I suppose you're right. But I'll tell you this much. Staying with them is an experience. Anyone who stays with them, even for a night, never forgets it."

"Now we are curious," Kay said.

* * *

The Fowlers took Danny and Kay back to the Guatemala City airport the following morning and stood there visiting until the plane was filled with gas and ready to go. Danny went into the administration building to file a flight plan. While he was gone, Phyllis and Kay had a cup of coffee in the cafe.

"It's so good to be back here," Kay said wistfully. "You know, Phyllis, this morning it almost seems as though we've never been away. Everything seems so familiar – so warm, friendly, and inviting."

"I know just what you mean. Everything here seems so real and everything else so far away."

They talked on until Kay saw that Danny was approaching. Then she stopped quickly and got to her feet. "Here comes Danny. I know he's going to be anxious to be going."

"Now remember, Kay, you're to come back to the city and stay with us a few days before you go back home."

"We'll try," she replied, "but why don't you plan on coming out to Cielo and see us while we're there. We'd love to have you."

Phyllis's face brightened. "I'd love to. Believe me, Kay, I'd enjoy nothing better than going to Cielo." Her eyes danced. "That's a thrill one doesn't get very often."

At that moment Danny reached them. About the same time Tow Fowler came from the other direction. It wasn't long until they climbed into the plane, taxied to the far end of the runway, and turned, waiting for the signal to take off.

Once they were airborne Danny banked sharply and brought the plane around to head up the coast. In little more than an hour and a half they reached the isolated Indian village of Cielo. The missionary pilot quickly spotted the airstrip that had been painstakingly hacked through the jungle and prepared to land.

"It's beautiful, isn't it?" he murmured.

"It–it's the most beautiful sight in all the world," Kay answered. Her voice choked.

Expertly Danny brought the plane down, landing on the narrow strip that had been cleared of trees. The villagers stood shyly along the landing strip, where they would remain as unobtrusive as possible.

"Look at them," Kay said, smiling at the sight. "I'd forgotten how shy they are – and how curious."

"So had I." He brought the plane to a stop by this time and was opening the cabin door. "I don't see the Davises, do you?"

Kay shook her head. "I thought I saw them just as we were landing, but I can't make them out now."

"They'll be along in a minute or two." Danny swung his legs around and climbed out of the plane. "There they are."

Even as he spoke a slender white man and his wife came hurrying forward.

"Welcome to Cielo." Gerald Davis thrust out his hand. Danny took it warmly. He introduced himself and Kay to Gerald and Rosalita Davis.

The Indians were moving closer, silently, their dark eyes studying the newcomers. Their faces were intent and unsmiling, neither friendly nor unfriendly, only very serious.

"You don't know how glad we are to have you here," Jerry Davis said.

"Or how thrilled we are to think that we're going to have an airplane stationed here," his wife added. "You don't know how desperately we've prayed for a plane."

"I only wish this one was going to be able to stay here permanently."

Jerry's smile flashed. "Well, we're thankful for the time it will be here. And thankful that you're here to fly it."

Jerry Davis was older than Danny by a number of years. Actually he looked almost old enough to have been Danny's father, although that could have been because of the way the tropics wore on him. That, and the fact that his hair had long since gone, leaving a fringe around the bottom and the top of his head completely bald. The relentless tropical sun had burned his face leather-brown and wrinkled it until he could have been any age. Yet there was a spring in his step that gave the impression he was about to break into a run at any moment, and the fire in his mild blue eyes commanded attention from everyone.

His wife, Rosalita, was one of those individuals who seems to grow more beautiful, more alive, and radiant with each passing year. Danny would not have guessed that she was almost the same age as her husband. She, too, was tanned dark by the sun. But her black hair and snapping eyes hinted, as much as her name, that she was of Spanish descent.

Jerry Davis spoke at last. "There's no need for us to stand out here. We might as well go to the house."

"I should tie down the aircraft first," Danny told him.

"I'll come back and help you take care of that afterwhile. Now we'd like to have you come to the house for a shower and something cool to drink."

"Fine. We'll get our luggage later, too."

As they approached the missionary's home, a handsome boy of eleven or twelve years came running out to meet them.

"Doug," Mr. Davis said, "this is Mr. and Mrs. Danny Orlis. Our son, Douglas."

The boy flashed a quick smile. "Want me to go and get your suitcases from the plane for you, Mr. Orlis?" he asked.

"That would be fine. Thank you."

With that, the boy scampered away.

They were just sitting down in the living room of the Davis home when the door opened and a boy came in. Danny looked up.

"That was a quick trip, Doug."

"A quick trip?" The boy's face crinkled quizzically. "I don't think I understand you, sir."

"You went after the luggage in the plane, didn't you?"

"Luggage?" The boy was still standing there, frowning. "Plane? I didn't go after any luggage anywhere."

"I–"

"You couldn't have told me to get your luggage," he continued. "I just got here this very minute."

Danny shook his head, bewildered. "Well, I told somebody to get our luggage. That's all I know."

CHAPTER 2

TRIPLE SURPRISE

It was a moment or two before Danny spoke again. When he did, bewilderment tinged his voice.

"Something strange is going on here. And whatever it is, I don't get it."

Jerry Davis's eyes were dancing, but he did not answer.

Danny got to his feet and walked to the screen door where he stood for a time looking out at the lush green foliage. A moment or two later a youngster appeared on the path.

"Oh, here comes another one."

A slim figure appeared at the door, and a thin, bronzed, young face smiled impishly up at him.

"Hi. Do you want me to go back to the plane and get your luggage?"

Danny opened the screen door.

"Maybe afterwhile, but right now I'd like to have a few words with you."

The youngster hesitated as though undecided whether to go into the house or whirl and dash away. The pilot decided the matter. He threw open the door and, leaping forward, clamped his hand on a wriggling young shoulder.

"Now, let's see who we have here." He jerked off the youngster's cap and a mass of heavy black hair tumbled out. "A girl! That's just what I thought. Now, who are you and just exactly what's going on here?"

She wriggled to free herself.

"That's not going to do you any good. You're not going to get away from me until you tell me what this is all about."

She giggled impishly. "I'm DeeDee."

"And who was that other character who looks exactly like you?"

"Which one?"

"Which one?" he echoed. "Was there more than one?"

"There were two." She was laughing until her sides shook. "That was Del and Doug you saw."

"Del and Doug?" The corners of Danny's mouth tightened. "That means there are at least three. How many of you are there, anyway?"

"How many do you think?" she demanded haughtily.

"I wouldn't guess. For all I know there may be a dozen."

"A dozen?" DeeDee laughed again. "There are only three of us. We're triplets."

"Triplets?" Danny joined the laughter. "That explains what everybody meant when they kept telling us we were in for a surprise when we got to Cielo."

"I thought everybody in the mission knew about the Davis triplets," Jerry Davis said. "The kids are well known for their pranks."

"You can say that again. Everybody in the mission has been telling us how much we were going to enjoy our stay at Cielo."

"I hope they were sincere," Rosalita said, "and not speaking in sarcasm."

"Nobody would find these kids anything but delightful," Kay assured her.

Jerry turned to his daughter.

"You'd better go and get those two scalawags who're always thinking up this mischief, and see that they bring Danny and Kay's luggage to the guesthouse."

"If you can find them," the triplets' mother put in.

"Oh, I can find them easy. They're just outside in the bush." She gestured with her hand. "They wanted to get in on the fun, too."

"Well, you've had your fun. Now, scoot. There's some work to do."

She flashed a quick, warm little smile at Danny and Kay and dashed out the door. When she was gone Rosalita looked over at Kay.

"I suppose we shouldn't let the children tease our guests so much." There was the faintest trace of a Spanish accent in her voice. "But they enjoy confusing strangers so much that we don't have the heart to spoil their little game."

Kay laughed pleasantly. "I think it's cute."

"So do I," Danny replied. "I'm a sucker for little brunettes about that age." He paused for a moment. "If DeeDee had her hair cut short, I'd really have been fooled. As it was, when I saw her hair peeking out from under her hat I couldn't quite figure out if I was seeing things or what."

"Rosalita and I had been married almost fourteen years when the triplets came along. They've been a tremendous blessing to us, believe me."

Danny was still laughing. "And," he said, "I'll bet they keep you young."

"I'll say they do."

Rosalita's smile faded. "They're not bad youngsters," she said defensively. "I wouldn't even say they're particularly naughty. At least they're no worse than a lot of other children their age. It's just that they've got so much life they can't sit still for an instant."

"Especially DeeDee," Jerry added. "I think she's at the bottom of most of the pranks they pull."

Rosalita fixed some cold fruit juice and served it. Danny was still talking about DeeDee and her brothers.

"You're going to have to be careful when we leave here or we're apt to have them in our suitcase. I don't think I've ever seen such cute youngsters."

Jerry nodded thoughtfully. "They sometimes create quite a problem for us. When we were home on our last furlough everybody made such a fuss over the kids, they got to thinking they were about the cutest things that ever happened. We had quite a job getting them back to normal."

At that moment Doug, Del, and DeeDee came back to the house with the luggage. DeeDee came in first and then her brothers. She was only slightly smaller than the boys. The difference was so slight that only when they stood together was Danny able to see it. The boys were exactly the same size. Their snapping black eyes were the same shade, their oval faces were the same, and their black hair was cut the same. They stood the same way, smiled the same, and talked the same.

Dolores, who was always called DeeDee, had long black hair. That and the minute difference in her size was all that set her apart from her brothers.

* * *

Danny and Kay were so tired the evening they arrived in Cielo that they excused themselves and went to bed early. When at last they got up, the sun was slanting into the window of the guesthouse bedroom.

"Danny, you can't say anything anymore to me about sleeping late," she said. "Look what time it is."

He stirred and opened one eye to squint at the clock.

"It is late. Why didn't you wake me?" He clambered out of bed and began dressing.

Kay laughed. "I didn't wake you because I was sleeping so soundly myself if you want to know the truth."

"That's exactly what I thought."

They got up and dressed hurriedly. They had been invited over to the Davis home for breakfast that morning. When they finally got there the triplets were nowhere in sight. Rosalita and Jerry greeted them warmly.

"I told Jerry I wasn't going to fix breakfast until you got here," Rosalita said. "We both remarked about how tired you looked last night."

"I didn't realize that it showed so much," Danny said.

Kay smiled. "I'll have to admit I was terribly tired last night, but today I feel wonderful." She took a deep breath. "I don't know when I've been so happy as I've been since we got back to Guatemala. I feel as though I've come back home."

"I know just what you mean," Mrs. Davis said. "When we've been on furlough, we feel the same way."

Jerry turned to Danny. "As soon as breakfast is over, I'd like to go out and really inspect that new airplane."

"I think we'll be able to do better than that. I'll give you a demonstration ride."

The older missionary smiled. "You'd better not let the kids hear you say that. Ever since they found out you were coming, they've been talking about getting a ride in that plane."

"We can probably take care of that, too. In fact, I think I'd enjoy it as much as they would."

They were still visiting when Rosalita called Danny and Kay to breakfast. Mr. and Mrs. Davis sat up at the table with them while they ate. After a time Rosalita turned to Danny.

"You don't know how much we've been praying for an airplane to help with the work here," she said. "Now that you've come, even for a short time, it seems almost like a dream."

"I'm sure it's going to be a great time-saver," he replied. "I've been told that in many areas a plane can make each missionary several times more effective than he would be without it."

Jerry laughed good-naturedly. "From the little experience we've had with aircraft, I'm sure that's true, but Rosalita is thinking about something a little different."

"That's right. I don't like these dugout canoes we have to use in some places to get from one village to another. They frighten me every time I get in them."

"I know exactly how you feel," Kay put in. "That was one of the things I dreaded more than anything else when we were here as missionaries. They're not only frightening, but it takes so long to get anywhere in one of them."

* * *

That afternoon Danny and Jerry went out to check the supply of aviation gas that had been brought in by boat the week before.

"Is this all the gas you've got, Mr. Davis?" There was concern in the young pilot's voice.

"That's all," he replied. "We ordered five hundred gallons, but when the boat came, they only had two barrels for us. That's typical of the situation out here, as you probably remember. It's a little better now than it used to be, but I feel fortunate if we get any of the things we order, let alone the exact quantity."

Danny grinned crookedly. "I was wondering what we were going to do first, but this settles that problem. We're going to have to ferry in some gas."

Jerry squinted at the aircraft that was glistening under the glazing sun.

"You won't have to make too many trips with that plane," he said. "She looks as though she'd haul a tremendous load."

"You can say that again. Six people and a thousand pounds. That's what should make her so valuable on the mission field. She's a real workhorse."

They walked over to the plane and the missionary pilot checked the ties.

"You aren't going down for gas yet this afternoon, are you?"

He shook his head. "No, I think I'll gas up and get the barrels washed out and loaded in the plane so we can take off the first thing in the morning."

They were just starting to work when one of the triplets popped out of the bush near the aircraft.

"Hi, Danny!" A broad grin split his handsome young face.

The pilot looked up. "Hello there."

"Bet you can't guess my name."

"I could guess it, but I don't know whether I could come up with the right one or not."

"Go ahead. Try."

Danny's eyes twinkled teasingly. "I know which one you are now," he said. "You're DeeDee."

"Aw–" Doug Davis wrinkled his nose. "You know better than that. You're just trying to have some fun with me. That's all."

"Isn't that what you did with me yesterday?"

At that moment Mr. Davis broke in. "How about getting Del and giving us a hand, Doug?" he suggested. "We've got some work to do."

With that the other boy peeked out from behind a clump of palmetto, eyes sparkling. "Are you lookin' for somebody, Dad?" he wanted to know.

"Yes, I'm looking for somebody, namely you. And if you don't get over here and give us a hand, you and I are going to be having some trouble. And that's for sure."

The boys approached the plane, eyeing it speculatively.

"We–we were sort of figuring on making a deal with Danny, Dad. About some of this work you're talking about."

"A deal?" Jerry's forehead crinkled with suspicion. "Now just what kind of a deal are you planning to make?"

"Like working for him if he'll give us a ride in the plane."

There was a short silence.

"You guys don't think the mission sent Danny all the way down here from Minneapolis to haul you two around, do you?"

The boys' eyes grew serious.

"But they don't want poor little missionary kids like Doug and me to sit here at Cielo all the time without ever havin' any fun, do they?"

"That's right, Dad," the other boy said quickly. "We're supposed to be happy, aren't we?"

"Sure, you're supposed to be happy. Danny and I both want you to be happy. That's why we're letting you help us clean these gas barrels and load them."

Doug hesitated. "No deal?"

"No deal." His dad's voice rose slightly. "But I can promise you that you'll have a big deal with me if you don't get to work pronto."

"Come on, Del," Doug said, "I think he means it."

Danny watched the two boys work together. It was quite apparent that, for all their teasing and good-natured bantering, they both knew how to work. And, what was more, there was real respect in their voices when they talked to their dad, even when they were clowning around.

Quite unexpectedly a new pain stabbed to the very

depths of Danny's being. If he had sons of his own, he would want them to be just like Doug and Del. They were happy and carefree; life was a new, exciting adventure for them, but they were serious, too, and gave every indication of being good, fun-loving Christian kids.

That night in the little grass-roofed guesthouse, he was still thinking about the triplets and mentioned them to Kay.

"What do you think of them?" he asked.

"They're darling." She giggled to herself, thinking about them. "But I don't know when I've seen kids so mischievous. What one of them can't think of the others do. They're priceless."

"They do have a good time, but if you've noticed, they don't do anything mean. It's all good, clean fun. They're so bright-eyed and bushy-tailed I think they'd explode if they didn't do something to let off steam."

There was a long, painful silence.

"When I see them, it makes me miss Kent and Jill more than ever," Kay said.

Danny nodded. "You know, if we had children of our own, I think I'd want them to be just like the Davis triplets."

"Oh, Danny!"

He laughed.

"Well, they'd sure keep a guy young."

"I suppose it depends on how you look at it."

CHAPTER 3

RETURNING ILLNESS

Danny started flying early the next morning. He hauled in two loads of aviation gas, a large load of supplies for the Davis family, and two loads of building material – all in three days. Jerry Davis shook his head in disbelief.

"I can't get over the amount of freight you've hauled in since you came, Danny," he said, "it just doesn't seem possible."

"I feel the same way, and I'm flying a 180 all the time. We couldn't begin to move the amount of stuff I've hauled in three days with the mission plane."

"I'm going to get started on that new building right away. I thought I'd have to wait at least two months for the building material to come up by boat. And I was prepared to wait twice that long because they usually forget half of it the first time." He smiled broadly. "I tell you, Danny, this plane is the finest thing that ever happened to this mission field. That's for sure."

"I have to agree with you. It's going to be a great thing for missionary work in a lot of hard places."

While Danny, Mr. Davis, and Doug and Del were unloading the last of the building material from the plane, DeeDee stood before the guesthouse door for a moment or two. She moved her hand as though to knock, hesitated, and raised it to knock again. Suddenly, she made up her mind and knocked timidly.

There was no answer.

DeeDee waited a moment or two. She acted as though she was about to leave, but stopped, brushed her hand lightly across her face, and turned back. Once more she paused uncertainly. She looked about and turned once more to push lightly on the door. It swung ajar.

"Kay!" she called. "Kay!"

She peered inside, but could see no one.

"Kay!"

There was a stirring in the bedroom as though someone was struggling to sit up.

"Kay!" she called again, moving further into the guesthouse and looking around.

"Who is it?" The voice was faint and far away.

"It's me. DeeDee." She walked to the bedroom door and stared inside. Kay was lying on the bed.

Her eyes widened. "What's the matter, Kay? Are you sick?"

Kay smiled wanly and once more tried to get to her feet. But she could not. She fell back, exhausted. For half a minute she lay there, breathing heavily. Her face was pale and colorless.

"Are you sick?" DeeDee repeated.

'I've just got a headache, that's all. I'll be all right in a little while."

The frightened girl came over to the bed and looked down at her tenderly.

"Oh, you look awful sick," she gasped. "I'd better go and get Mom."

Horror leaped to Kay's eyes. "No!" she exclaimed, grasping DeeDee's arm tightly. "Please! I'm all right! I've just got a little headache. That's all. I'll be all right in a little while." She struggled to sit up.

"I–I should go and get Mom to help you. She knows about everything." Her expression changed. "Or almost everything."

"If I was really sick, I'd let you go and get your mother, DeeDee. But I'm not." This time she managed to swing her feet over the side of the bed. For a time she sat there, breathing heavily. Then she grasped the nightstand beside the bed and pulled herself up. "Don't worry your mother about me. She has so much to do that's really important without coming over here to look after me. I'll be all right."

She walked slowly into the kitchen. The girl followed her.

"The boys wanted me to go out to the plane with

them," she said, "but I told them I'd rather come over here and see you."

"I'm glad you did." Kay made her way in the direction of the refrigerator. "Would you like some cold pineapple juice, DeeDee?"

As she spoke, she reached out to open the refrigerator door, but for an instant, all went black. Her head reeled and she grasped frantically for support.

DeeDee sprang to her side.

"What is it, Kay?" she cried, her voice betraying her concern. "What's the matter?"

"I–I'm all right." She straightened with considerable effort and ran an uncertain hand across her moist forehead. "I must have gotten up too soon. I–I got dizzy all of a sudden."

She started to move.

"Here, let me help you."

Kay motioned DeeDee aside and stumbled over to a chair where she sat down heavily. Her eyes were glazed and her whole body seemed to tremble. The frightened girl stared numbly at her. It was a moment or two before Kay could speak. When she did there was a strange tone to her voice.

"I can't figure out what happened to me," she murmured at last. "It's been years since I've felt that way."

She checked herself suddenly. It had, indeed, been years since she felt that way. It had been years since that terrible day in the dugout canoe. She had felt the same way then; that terrible day when she got so sick, they had to leave their work in Guatemala and go back to Minnesota.

She had felt so good the last few years that she had been hoping against hope she wouldn't have any more trouble with heat exhaustion. She had been hoping, although she hadn't even dared to mention it to Danny, that she might be over it now so they could go back to Guatemala as missionaries once again. The barb stabbed deeply into her heart. Was it going to happen again?

DeeDee was still standing there, her fright reflected in her dark eyes.

Kay pulled in a thin breath and expelled the air slowly. "I–I think I feel better now."

"Are you sure?"

Kay smiled and nodded. "It wasn't anything. Really."

There was a brief pause.

"DeeDee, I wonder if I could trust you to keep a secret for me?"

The girl nodded. "Whatever it is, I won't tell."

"Don't say anything to anyone about my getting sick. I mean about–about this. I'm afraid Danny will get all upset about it, and it isn't anything."

DeeDee hesitated. "Mom could probably give you something so it wouldn't happen again."

"It isn't going to happen again. If it does, I'll tell your mother about it myself. How's that?"

* * *

Once the supplies and building material had been ferried to Cielo, Danny and Jerry began to visit the villages that had clearings large enough to serve as airstrips.

"It's too bad we don't have more places to land," Danny said. "If we did, we'd be able to visit all of your outpost stations."

"I only wish every village in our territory had a landing strip, Danny," Jerry said fervently. "If they did, we'd be able to do three months' work in a week."

"I'm not sure whether the mission is going to be able to base a plane down here or not," Danny replied, "but if they should, wouldn't it be easy to convince the people that they ought to clear landing strips?"

"I'm sure they would if we presented the idea to them in the right way. A plane would be of real service to the people in case of emergency."

After a time Danny opened his bag and got out his air maps. "Where do you want to go tomorrow, Jerry?"

The missionary studied the map thoughtfully for a time.

"Actually, we're going to have to be governed by the places we can land. There aren't very many places that are even close to landing strips. I don't think there are more than half a dozen close enough to places where we can land for the plane to do us any good."

He pulled up a chair and leaned forward to study the map with Danny.

"When I fly north, the missionaries usually like to use the plane to get to places that are the least accessible or those they haven't visited for quite a while."

Jerry nodded thoughtfully. "Usually that's the same place," he said. After a minute or more he pointed to a settlement up the river. "We could go to Castillo. It's right on the river and is quite an important village. There's a landing strip there."

"Good."

"For some reason Indians from other settlements are always visiting there. In fact, it's only been a couple of years since Rosalita and I got so excited about the possibilities of opening a new work there that we considered asking the mission to transfer us. I think we'd probably be living at Castillo right now if the people here hadn't been so anxious to have us stay."

Danny frowned. "Did you say there's a landing strip there?"

"As I recall, it's very adequate. The government had it cut in so they could fly supplies to the area when the army was operating there."

"That's fine. Castillo sounds as though it's as good a place as any to start with. We can fly in, stay for a couple of days, and do visitation or whatever fits into your schedule. Then we can go on to another settlement."

Jerry turned to stare directly at Danny, a curious light flickering in his eyes. "I can't get over how simple and easy you make that sound."

"It is simple, and it's certainly not very hard," Danny continued. "We probably won't be in the air more than thirty minutes going to Castillo. It's no sweat at all! As soon as we get up in the air, we'll start thinking about landing."

There was a brief silence.

"I don't know whether I'll ever be able to get used to this air travel or not. I've been out here too long and have had to depend too much on dugout canoes and horseback or going on foot."

"You'll adjust to it quickly, believe me."

"Maybe so, but I've got to admit I'm completely floored by the idea of getting into these villages as easily as we're talking about doing right now. It doesn't even seem possible."

Danny laughed. "Wait until tomorrow. I'll show you exactly how easy it is to get to Castillo by air – especially in a plane like this."

"I suppose you're right, but if we were to go up to Castillo from here by canoe, we'd have at least a week of hard, dangerous going." He shook his head. "And you talk about doing it in a matter of minutes. It's fantastic!"

"But very possible – and safe. This plane is going to make it possible for one missionary to reach three or four times as many people as before. And make life much easier and safer for the missionaries, too."

"You can say that again." Jerry's expression changed. "I can think of several American and European missionaries and their children who would be alive today if there had been a plane out here to get them to a doctor when they first got sick."

Danny excused himself and went back to the guesthouse. He had thought Kay would be waiting up for him, but she was already in bed. He went quickly to the bedroom and looked in.

"What's the matter?" he asked quickly. "Don't you feel well, Kay?"

She did not answer him immediately.

"Don't you feel well?" he repeated.

"I got so tired this afternoon I felt that I just had to go to bed early tonight."

He pulled up a chair and sat down beside the bed.

"I didn't think you looked well at noon today. What seems to be the trouble?" Concern edged his voice.

"I don't think there's anything much wrong with me. I've had a headache and have been dizzy and tired the last day or so. I think I've just had a touch of the flu."

Danny was a long while in answering. "I hope that's all it is. I certainly hope so."

CHAPTER 4

AMONG THE INDIANS

The following morning Danny and Jerry were up before daylight. They topped off the fuel tanks and loaded the gear into the aircraft while Rosalita was getting their clothes ready in the house.

"There," the missionary said, shoving the last sleeping bag into the cargo compartment and straightening it. "That does it."

Danny looked over the load quickly to be sure that it was all tied down and wasn't going to be bouncing dangerously in the plane in case they encountered rough flying weather.

"I guess everything's all right," he said at last. "I'll loosen these ties and we'll be ready to start the engines and take off."

The pilot stooped to untie the knots, but a wiry twelve-year-old beat him to it.

"Here, Danny," Doug exclaimed, "let me do that for you."

Danny stared at him. "What's going on here?" he asked suspiciously.

Del was on the other side, loosening the ties over there. "What's this all about?"

"We just came down to help you," Del explained.

Dark eyes looked impudently up at Danny. "Aren't we nice?" Doug asked.

The missionary pilot laughed. "I don't know about that. When I start getting help from characters like you two, I begin to suspect something. What's your angle?"

They frowned innocently.

"See, Doug, I told you it wouldn't work. I told you Danny would just get suspicious."

Their dad joined in. "Danny isn't the only one who's getting suspicious. I'm trying to figure out what you two are trying to get for yourselves."

"Oh, we don't want anything for ourselves." Suddenly Doug's eyes danced as though he had just made an outstanding discovery. "Unless you'd really like to take us with you as a little reward for all the good things we've done for you."

Del spoke up quickly. "That's a great idea, Doug. The airplane will hold six people, and they're not going to be hauling any freight. That would make plenty of room for two tiny little guys like us." He turned to Danny. "You'd really like to make us happy by taking us with you, wouldn't you?"

Jerry spoke first, before Danny had an opportunity to do so.

"Not this time, guys," he said. "We've got a lot of work to do. And besides, you've got your chores to take care of."

"DeeDee would do our chores for us while we were gone," Doug told him. He eyed Jerry critically to see if there was any sign of weakening, but there was none. Their dad only shook his head.

The two men climbed into the plane and Danny started the engines. When the gauges indicated the oil and engine heat were at the proper temperature, Danny taxied to the far end of the runway and turned the aircraft around. Then he and Gerald bowed their heads for a word of prayer before taking off. The flight over the sparsely populated forest was short and pleasant. In less than half an hour the village of Castillo appeared on the horizon.

"There's where we're headed, Danny," Jerry said. "You hit it right on the button."

The young missionary pilot grinned. "Navigating on a day like this is a breeze. It's when the weather gets sticky that a guy begins to wonder whether he ever learned anything about navigating."

They nosed down toward the narrow landing strip that had been slashed through the lush forest.

"I don't think we'll go in this time," he observed. "I'm going to make a pass over it first to see what it's like. Then if it looks okay, we'll come around and land."

"The government's been using it right along, so I think it must be all right."

"I'm sure it is," Danny answered, "but I would rather take a look at it than commit ourselves to landing and find out when it's too late that there's something wrong with the strip."

Danny cut the speed and flew over the landing strip as close to the treetops as was safe. The strip looked rough, but in good shape otherwise. He banked sharply and brought the trim twin-engine craft about in a sweeping semicircle and landed near the village.

"Look," Jerry said, pointing at the Indians clustered along the landing strip a discreet distance away. "We've got an audience."

"Wherever we go out here we have people gather to watch us," Danny said. "It doesn't make much difference whether they're brown or white."

The two men got out of the plane and approached the villagers. Jerry spoke to them in their own dialect. The sound of their native tongue brought faint smiles to their faces. A number of them murmured a greeting.

A slight, mahogany-skinned man took a step forward and spoke earnestly with the missionary. Danny could not understand what he said, but it was apparent that he was the chief. One had only to note his regal bearing to see that he was the headman in the village.

"He welcomes us to his village," the missionary interpreted to Danny. "He says that he remembers

Rosalita and me from our other visits here several years ago. He says that he knows we are friends of his and his people, so we are free to come and go as we wish."

"That's great."

"It's an answer to prayer. You know from your time out here that the chief rules his village with an iron hand. What he says goes. And if he orders a person to stay out of his village, he'd better stay out."

Danny nodded.

The chief waited until the two of them had finished talking. Then he spoke again. Jerry answered him, and for several minutes they carried on an animated conversation. After several minutes he glanced at his companion. "Danny, get my bag. We have his permission to talk to the people."

Everything in the Guatemalan rainforest moved at a leisurely pace. Jerry knew that well. He took his time getting out his tablet, and when he spoke, it was slowly, as though the clock no longer existed. Even then he did not give the lesson immediately. To have started preaching at once would have been a terrible breach of good manners. There had to be talk first, the polite exchange of pleasantries. Danny and the veteran missionary squatted in the shade of the towering trees and Jerry visited with the people. Every now and then he would pause and interpret for Danny.

At last he sensed that propriety had been served and that he was free to proceed. Slowly, and with great feeling, he began to tell the story of Noah and the ark. As he talked, the crowd grew larger and larger. At first Danny was thrilled to see such interest on the part of everyone. Then he realized that much of it was only curiosity. The crowd had gathered simply to hear what these two strange men had come to tell them. They had no understanding of what Jerry was trying so desperately to say to them. And what was worse, they didn't particularly care to know. It satisfied them to hear the words, to observe the strange things this white man was doing.

As the missionary spoke Danny prayed silently that the hearers would be able to understand and would heed the message they were hearing – most of them for the first time in their lives.

Although Jerry must have been more aware of their indifference than Danny, there was no indication of it in his tone or the sparkle in his eyes. He continued with the lesson about Noah. In great detail he described the wickedness of the people and told that God had sent the flood to destroy the world because of it.

The crowd continued to grow as men and women sauntered by. Already all the children in the settlement were crowded closely about Jerry, their dark faces serious as they considered every word. The older ones gathered too, but more slowly, and with a certain amount of reticence. They were attracted by the sight of the strange white man who spoke their language as well as they did themselves and had pictures of all kinds of animals.

One such young man, dressed in baggy trousers and a brilliantly colored shirt, pushed his way to the front and hunkered down among the children, almost at the missionary's feet. His dark eyes were riveted fixedly on Jerry's face.

The story was finally finished. Jerry paused. He wouldn't give an invitation. Few knowledgeable missionaries in that area did. He would wait, praying that God would speak to hearts. Then the people would come to him, and he could talk with them about their personal need for a Savior. Until that happened, he could only wait.

The young man who listened so seriously got to his feet, but he did not leave immediately. Instead he paused. Jerry saw his indecision and paused too.

"Greetings," the missionary said.

"Greetings." The voice was hesitant and reserved, but to the trained ear it was also friendly. He acted as though he wanted to talk but did not feel that he should open the conversation.

"Your clothes say that you are from another village," Jerry ventured.

"From up the river, I come."

There was a brief pause.

"Have you ever heard the story before?"

The Indian shook his head.

"Nobody ever tell us anything like that in our village," he said.

Although the missionary did not reply immediately, he remained motionless, reluctant to leave.

"Did you understand what you heard?"

"No." The Indian frowned. "Nim Ajaw, he is our god. He looks after our people and, if it pleases him, he gives us good crops."

The missionary chose his words with great care lest he offend the man who stood before him. He did not criticize the Indian's god. He did not tell him that it was useless to worship such a creature. That would come later, after he had made friends with the man – after he had won his confidence. Now he avoided mentioning Nim Ajaw and spoke of God.

"The God I worship sent His Son to die on the cross for our sin so we can go to heaven," he went on softly, in a tone that befitted one who was talking to such gentle, well-mannered people. "He made a way for us to escape, so we won't be lost like the wicked people who were drowned in the terrible flood."

The Indian turned the matter over in his mind. He did not speak of that at the moment. It was something to be pondered, something to be studied over when a man was alone on the trail. And, perhaps, it was something to be discussed in secret by the elders in the village, away from the ears of the women and children who might so easily be led astray. As he thought, his face was inscrutable.

"Never have I heard such things," he admitted, awe creeping into his voice. "Never have I heard of One who can get a man to heaven."

"Think on what we have talked about. Think well."

The Indian nodded and started away, but after a moment he turned and came back.

"You tell the story again?" he asked.

Danny would not have been surprised had Jerry put him off until the following morning – or at least until that night when he would have a chance of getting another crowd around, but he did not. Smiling, he got out the computer once more and began to relate the story in as much detail as though he had a hundred in his audience instead of one.

The Indian stared silently as the missionary related the story. He clung hungrily to every word that was spoken. So intent was he that he was not even mindful of Danny or the inevitable children who saw what was happening and came back to watch. When Jerry finished, the Indian stood tall and, without a word, turned and started away. The missionary called after him.

"If you come back tomorrow," he said, "I'll tell you another story."

There was no indication that the Indian had even heard what he said.

The next day, however, Danny and Jerry were just finishing breakfast when there was a polite cough at the door. The missionary went to answer it. It was the same Indian who had shown such interest in the story the day before.

"Greetings," Jerry said.

The Indian did not reply but stalked into the

guesthouse. Danny smiled warmly at him, but the man acted as though he didn't even see him.

"Is there something I can do for you?" the missionary asked.

"You come to my village and tell story?" he asked. There was a wistful tone in his voice. "You come and tell about the people being wicked and God sending all the water? You come and tell about the animals?"

"If I can." Again there was a hesitation. "By what name do you call your village?"

"Pieto."

Jerry nodded. "Pieto. I have heard of that village. It is a village of good hunters."

The Indian accepted the compliment without reply. "It is two, maybe three hours from here by canoe."

The missionary got Danny's map and, with the Indian's help, marked the obscure little village on the river a dozen or more miles upstream.

"You think the people would like to hear the story at Pieto?" he asked.

The Indian nodded. "I tell them about it. They like to hear." Fear forced the interest from his eyes. "You come?" His voice quavered. "You come to tell us?"

"We'll come if we possibly can."

When the Indian was gone Danny turned quickly to his missionary companion. "This is tremendous. Do you think you'll be able to get up to his village and follow up on his people?"

There was a deep longing in Jerry's voice.

"I certainly hope so. A contact like this one is something that doesn't happen very often. When it comes, I take it as coming from the Lord and try to do everything I can to exploit it."

Danny pulled in a deep breath. "I don't know when I've seen anyone so interested in the story of Noah as he was."

"We had his attention, all right."

"After the interest he showed yesterday, I wouldn't have been at all surprised this morning if he'd made a decision for Christ."

A grin lifted the corner of the missionary's mouth. "I could have gotten him to make a decision if I'd pressed him a little," he went on, "but I didn't feel that he was ready. He doesn't have enough understanding of what it's all about. I'm afraid he'd have been 'unripe fruit.' He's going to have to do some serious thinking about the things he heard yesterday and then weigh them against the religion of his people. It isn't the sort of thing that happens overnight."

Danny nodded to indicate that he understood the situation. "But I'm sure the day will come when that young man will decide for Christ."

Danny went over and got the coffeepot, but he wasn't thinking about breakfast. He was thinking about the desperate longing in the young Indian's face.

CHAPTER 5

DANGEROUS TRIP

The next afternoon Danny and Jerry flew back to the mission station. By the time they had the plane tied down, they were making plans to return to Castillo and Pieto.

"I'd like to have you make the trip with us, Danny," Jerry continued, "but it's really a waste of your valuable time to have you traveling by canoe when you could be flying to the other stations and accomplishing so much more."

"I think I have to agree with you, but I still don't like the idea of your making the trip from Castillo to Pieto alone, that's all."

"That isn't anything new to me. I've gone alone lots of times."

By now they had reached the house. Rosalita heard snatches of the conversation.

"What are you two talking about?"

Jerry told her about the lessons and the young man who listened to it twice and wanted them to come to his village and tell the same story to the people.

"We were trying to figure out the best way of following up on it," he told her. "I really believe that young man could be brought to the Lord if we could talk to him once more."

His wife's eyes sparkled with excitement. "Oh, that sounds wonderful!" she exclaimed. "The Lord must be answering our prayers for that area, Jerry. You know, we were praying about going up there a year or so ago."

Danny turned to Rosalita. "I was trying to convince Jerry that I ought to go in with him, but he doesn't think so."

"Neither do I," she spoke up quickly.

"You mean you're against me too?"

"What I mean is that if anybody goes with Jerry to Pieto, I'm going along."

They all ate dinner together that evening. As soon as they finished eating, the triplets went off to bed. The talk around the table was still about the village of Pieto.

"You know, Danny," Jerry continued, "we shouldn't let too much time go by before we make contact again."

"Just say the word and we'll go back – as far as Castillo, anyway."

For a while Jerry was silent. When he finally spoke there was a serious tone to his voice.

"I'd like to go in as soon as we can. Within a couple of days, at the most."

"You're going to take me with you, aren't you, Jerry?" his wife asked.

"It sounds as though I'll have to."

"You know what the attitude of the men will be if I'm along. They're going to think you have a peaceful purpose in mind or you wouldn't take me along. I know they're friendly enough so there isn't any danger on that score."

Jerry glanced at Danny and winked.

"I don't know about that."

"Besides, if we're going to move into that area, I ought to start getting acquainted with the women. We don't want to waste any time making friends with the people."

Rosalita stopped abruptly and glanced at Kay.

"There's something I hadn't thought of until right now. We have the triplets and no one to take care of them – unless you and Danny would."

"That would be wonderful," Kay exclaimed.

"It certainly would," Danny said.

"I was telling Jerry the other night that the triplets seem to like you two better than anyone else we've ever met."

Kay smiled. "We'll be happy to take care of them. In fact, it'll be a privilege."

That night when Danny and Kay were finally back in the guesthouse alone, they were still talking about the triplets.

"It's going to be good to have them with us for a little while, isn't it, Danny?"

"It sure is." Then concern crept into his voice. "I hope it works out all right."

"What do you mean? I thought you enjoyed having them around."

"I do. In fact, I don't see how anyone could help liking them." He paused significantly.

"Only–"

"Only what?"

"I was just thinking that taking care of them might be a little too much for you."

Kay's face paled and for half a minute she could not speak.

"I don't know why you would think that," she replied lamely.

"Maybe I'm getting upset over nothing, but when we came in this afternoon, you looked so pale it bothered me. You didn't look as though you felt well at all."

Kay managed a thin smile. "I believe the kids are just what I need to get my mind off myself," she continued. When she saw that there was still concern in Danny's eyes, she stopped. "I have had a few headaches," she admitted, "but they haven't been anything to get upset about. Besides, I haven't had any for the last couple of days. I feel all right now."

He still was not satisfied. "Kay, if you get to feeling bad, you'll tell me about it right away, won't you?"

"I'll tell you," she answered. "I promise."

The lines in Danny's forehead deepened. "I don't mind telling you I haven't felt at all easy about your coming down here with me. I've been afraid the same thing would happen that happened before."

"But that was years ago."

"I know, but the mission doctor wouldn't let us come back because of it. He said you were apt to have the same trouble again if you came down into this heat."

"Well, don't worry about it," she retorted. "I'm all right and I'm going to continue to be all right. You'll see."

For a minute or two neither of them spoke. Finally, Danny broke the silence.

"It's going to be good to have the triplets with us, even for a little while."

She brightened noticeably. "I know I'm being selfish, but I keep wishing that it was for longer than just a week."

"So do I, but we should be thankful that we're going to have them that long."

* * *

The next day Jerry and Rosalita rushed frantically to get ready for their trip. They packed their sleeping bags, blankets, mosquito netting, and some extra clothes in their duffle bags. Then they got some food together. Rosalita washed some extra clothing for the triplets.

"I'm glad you're going to move in here with the kids, Kay," she said the afternoon before they were to go. "It will be so much easier than it would be for us to haul all of their things over to the guesthouse."

At that moment Doug stuck his head in the kitchen door. "Hi, Mom. Hi, Kay. Where's Dad?"

"I think he and Danny are putting gas in the airplane. They said something about taking care of that this afternoon."

The boy entered the kitchen and sat down near the table.

"Now what's on your mind?" Rosalita asked knowingly.

His eyes were innocent. "What makes you think there's something on my mind?" he asked.

"I just know you. That's all."

It was a minute or so before he spoke.

"How about taking me along to Pieto, Mom? Would that be okay?"

"I don't think there's room."

"The plane's big enough to haul six people and there'll only be three of you. There'll be plenty of room for a skinny little guy like me."

"Dad said something about some freight they're supposed to haul to Castillo for the chief."

Doug was crestfallen. "And there won't even be room for me?"

"I'm afraid not."

"Aw—"

He was still sitting there some twenty minutes later.

"You'd just as well run along and find something to do, Doug," his mother told him. "You aren't going to get to go with us this time."

He shuffled out of the kitchen, dejection in every move.

It wasn't long until the door opened once more and a young voice piped, "Hi, Mom. Have you seen Doug anywhere around?"

She did not look up. "He was here a little while ago. Why?"

He came into the kitchen. "How about taking me along to this new village you and Dad are going to visit? I could help pole the dugout and carry your gear and everything."

"I just told Doug that we didn't have room for anyone else. We're carrying some supplies to Castillo for the chief. I–I–" She checked herself. "Wait a minute, you rascal! What do you mean by trying to fool me? You are Doug!"

He grinned impishly. "I just wanted to see if Del would have gotten the same answer I got," he said. "I wanted to see if you treat us the same."

His mother's voice rose indignantly. "You'd better get out of here before I whale you a couple."

He flashed her a quick smile that softened her heart and then scampered out into the bright sunlight.

Kay laughed. "Does this sort of thing happen very often?"

"More often than you'd think. They're always trying to fool us. And once in a while, if we don't watch closely, they're able to get away with it. Then they really think that they've done something."

The following morning Danny and his passengers were up an hour before dawn and had breakfast. As soon as it was daylight they took off.

At Castillo, Danny carried the missionary couple's gear down to the river while Jerry haggled with an Indian who knew the stream well enough to take them up to the settlement of Pieto.

"The river, she is very dangerous. It is worth much money to risk the swift water."

"It must not be so swift," the missionary countered. "Look. The children play in their dugouts on it."

"That is at Castillo," the would-be guide protested. "Up the river the water is swift."

"Your chief told me you would take us. Is it to be said that you are afraid?"

The Indian pretended to be furious. He brought up objection after objection. The price would have to be higher because there were two of them, and because only one would be able to help with the paddling. There were rapids on the river, and some dangerous snakes swam in it. The Indian boasted that he was not afraid, but that all such hazards required an increased fee. Nobody would take the risks of the river for the price Jerry offered. It was better to sit at home and watch the women work.

Jerry knew that haggling over the price was a favored pastime of the people. He also knew what a fair wage was. When, at last, he got the man down to a fair day's pay for the trip, he nodded in agreement.

The Indian was satisfied, too. Danny could tell by his manner. He knew what the man was thinking. He had gotten the white man up from a miserable wage to what a man should work for.

Once he was sure the bargaining was over, Danny went down to the river's edge. "I'll be back here for you in a week. Okay?"

Jerry nodded. "That sounds fine to me."

The Indian broke in quickly. "We go now. We get to Pieto before dark tonight."

Rosalita got into the dugout and took her place near the center.

"Take care of the kids for us."

"We'll do that," Danny assured her. "Don't worry about them. We'll have a great time with them."

With that the Indian thrust his pole into the mud, and the canoe moved slowly out into the river. Jerry and Rosalita both waved at Danny.

He stood on shore and watched until they rounded the bend and were out of sight. Then he turned and went back to the plane.

CHAPTER 6

TRAGEDY STRIKES

Danny waited until the chief and his men had unloaded the freight he brought for them. Then he took off, flew upstream until he saw Jerry and his wife and their guide in the needlelike dugout, and circled them. They waved as he flew over them and headed for the mission station. The flight back to Cielo was short and uneventful, very much like most of the flying he did back in the States. The only big difference was that the landings were trickier on the narrow, hand-hewn landing strips, especially if there happened to be a crosswind. But the problems were nothing he couldn't handle.

The Indians at Cielo had long since stopped coming out to the plane to watch every time it came in. But Doug and Del were another matter. They could always be counted on to listen for the airplane and be at the landing strip. He had never yet seen them before he touched the ground, but let the plane roll to a stop and there they were, stepping out of the bush near the place where he tied the aircraft down. Occasionally DeeDee was along.

That afternoon was no different than the others. He saw the two boys as he taxied to a stop and got out.

"Hi," he called, waving to them.

"Hi." Their voices were as somber as their eyes. He had never seen them look so serious.

At first he thought it was some sort of a gag – something like some of the other things they had pulled on him on other occasions.

"Now what's the trouble?" he asked. But, even as he spoke, he saw that this time they weren't joking.

"Kay's sick."

Danny caught his breath sharply. "Kay's sick?" he echoed. "What's the matter with her?"

"I don't know for sure," Del said. "DeeDee's with her. She's been putting cold towels on Kay's head, but I don't know what good anything like that does."

Danny quickly tied down the aircraft and started through the bush in the direction of the Davis home. Cold compresses were the treatment the doctor had recommended for Kay the time before when she had suffered from heat exhaustion. He didn't know how DeeDee could have known about that sort of treatment unless Kay had told her. Danny was running by the time he got to the house. He rushed to the bedroom and stopped just inside the door, staring down at his sick wife.

"What's the matter, Kay?"

At first she did not answer him. He moved slowly to the bed where he pulled up a chair and sat down.

"What's wrong?" he asked again.

She was a long time in answering. "At first I kept telling myself that this was just a headache, and that I'd get over it in a little while; but, Danny, there's no use in trying to kid myself any longer."

He spoke quietly. "It's the old heat exhaustion, isn't it?" he asked.

She nodded. And when she continued, her lips were trembling. "Ever since we began to plan our trip down here, Danny," she went on, "I've been thinking that perhaps God was going to let us come back here to serve Him. I figured that was the reason He took Kent and Jill from our home. With Jim away at school next fall, we wouldn't have any reason for not being here." She took a deep breath. "I could see everything working in that direction. But, almost as soon as we got here, I began to feel sick again."

He reached out and took her hand in his. "You haven't looked at all well for the last several days."

"I haven't been, Danny." She swallowed hard. "I'm certain now that God has permanently closed the door to our serving here."

He squeezed her hand reassuringly. "I'm glad you realize that, Kay. I've known for a long while that something has been bothering you. I wasn't sure what it was. Now I hope you're able to put it away."

She lay back and closed her eyes, breathing heavily. "I don't know why it is, Danny, but just having you here makes me feel better."

"If I'd known you were so sick, I'd have come back sooner, I can tell you that much." He got to his feet. "Whose idea was it to apply the cold packs?"

"I remembered what they did for me when I had heat exhaustion the other time."

At that moment DeeDee put another cold towel on Kay's head.

"I think I'm going to leave you alone for a little while," Danny said. "It would be better for you to try to sleep."

He left the room quietly. DeeDee followed him.

"I'm so glad you got back, Danny," she said, her young voice tremoring. "We were scared. The boys and I were awful scared."

Danny patted her on the shoulder, reassuringly.

"You've done a great job of taking care of her, DeeDee," he said. "I don't believe a registered nurse could have done any better."

The girl looked up at him, admiration and concern mingling in her eyes.

"What are you going to do, Danny? Take her back to the States?"

"She can't stay in this hot climate very long," Danny replied, "that's for sure." He spoke carefully. "But I don't know whether I'll have to take her home right away or not."

"We've sure been praying for her."

"We appreciate that, too." Danny crossed the kitchen floor and looked out the window for a moment. At last he turned back. "You kids handled this emergency the way things like this have to be handled. I know your parents are going to be very proud of you when I tell them about it."

That night Danny lay awake for several hours trying to decide what to do. At last he decided to fly Kay back to Guatemala City the next day and get her on a plane for the States. He could take the triplets with him, so he wouldn't have the worry of leaving them at Cielo alone.

The next day, however, was cloudy and cooler, and she seemed to feel a little better. Kay was able to come to the table for her meals.

"It's sure good to see you up today," he said. "You look as though you feel a little better."

She smiled wanly. "I do, but I still feel terribly weak."

"I was afraid I was going to have to take you to Guatemala City and send you back to the States this morning, the way you looked last night."

"I didn't say anything about it, but I was afraid of the same thing."

"Do you think it would be all right for you to stay until Jerry and Rosalita get back?"

"Oh, I think so. If it stays like this, I'm sure that I won't have any more trouble."

Danny breathed deeply. "I don't know how much longer I'll have to stay here myself. I've made several reports to the home board on the operation of the plane. Actually, I can see no point in testing it much further. It's checked out excellent in every phase of the work. As far as I'm concerned, I'm convinced that it not only will do the job, but that it's the coming plane for this area."

"It would be nice if we could go back to the States together."

Fortunately, the weather stayed cool for the next two or three days and Kay's condition improved slightly. She was even able to do some of the work around the house. Yet, it was apparent that she was still not well. Her color was bad, and there was a certain listlessness about her that normally wasn't there. And she seemed to require much more sleep than she normally needed.

Because the Davises would have to be brought out from Castillo before long and because Kay was still sick and needed him, Danny remained close to the mission station. He flew only to those places where he would be able to get back by nightfall.

Kay and the triplets had gone to bed, and he was sitting at the kitchen table reading his Bible when there was a noise at the back door. Curious, he went and opened it. In the darkness he could just make out the shadowy figure of an Indian man.

"Hello."

"You are Señor Orlis, no?"

"Sí. Won't you come in?"

The Indian did not move. Great emotion twisted his dark features.

"Bad thing happen!" he exclaimed. "Very bad!"

"Where? Where do you call home? Where do you live?"

"Chief, he send me to tell you."

Danny's lithe body stiffened. "What do you mean?"

"Canoe, she–" He made a quick, turning motion with his hands. "Señor Davis, he gone. Wife, she gone. Chief say you bring flying bird. Come quick!"

Danny stared incredulously into the somber face of the Indian. It wasn't true! It couldn't be! There had to be some mistake!

For a minute Danny did not move. An icy numbness stole through his body, sapping his strength and leaving him weak and trembling.

"You–you mean Mr. Davis and his wife are hurt?"

The Indian's gaze was still fastened on him. "Hurt?" He mouthed the word as though he wasn't sure just what it meant. "Canoe hit log." He made the flipping motion with his hands again. "They gone."

By this time Kay had heard the voices and, slipping into a robe, came into the kitchen.

"Who is it, Danny?" She stopped suddenly as she saw her young husband's ashen face. "What happened?"

"I'm not sure." He spoke slowly. "Apparently there's been an accident at Castillo."

The Indian nodded vigorously. "Sí. Accident. Accident. Chief say you should bring flying bird and come quick."

"I can't do that until it gets light," the pilot protested.

Kay looked up into Danny's saddened eyes. "Danny." Her voice choked. "Danny, do you suppose the Davises are–are–" She could not finish.

Danny put an arm around her shoulders. "I don't know what's happened. I can't understand all of his words." He pointed to the young Indian. "But it involves the Davises, and it sure sounds bad."

It was Kay who saw the great weariness in the Indian's face. "Oh, you poor man. Come in and sit down. I'll fix you something to eat."

The Indian allowed himself to be guided to the table and be seated. Only then did Kay and Danny realize that he had made the long trip without stopping for rest or food.

Kay got him something to eat – one of the Indian dishes she had learned to make. It was a favorite of the Davis triplets, and they kept the refrigerator well stocked with its simple ingredients, which they gleaned from the surrounding jungle.

While the man ate, Danny tried to find out more about the accident. But there seemed to be little more that the runner could tell. Jerry and Rosalita and an Indian guide had gone upstream from Pieto to visit a fishing camp where several of the men were staying. On the way back something must have happened. The canoe had floated down to Pieto and lodged against the shore at a bend in the river. There was no sign of the occupants.

Hope gleamed briefly in Kay's eyes. "Danny, they

could have gotten ashore after the canoe overturned, couldn't they?"

He nodded thoughtfully. "There's always that possibility, I suppose. The way the jungle is along the river it would be almost impossible for them to walk back to the village. Without the canoe they might have to stay where they are and wait until someone comes along." He pulled in a long, deep breath. "That's why it's important that I get up there as soon as it gets light."

CHAPTER 7

SEARCH FOR LIFE

Kay fixed a bed for the exhausted Indian runner and came back to the kitchen where Danny was still sitting at the table staring off into space. She pushed her hair back from her face with a trembling hand.

"Should we waken the children and tell them, Danny?" she asked.

He shook his head. "That wouldn't do any good. There's nothing anyone can do until morning. We'd just as well let them get a good night's sleep." He paused momentarily. "This might be the last untroubled sleep they'll get for a long while."

She sat down across from him. Suddenly all her strength seemed to be gone.

"What do you plan to do?"

Thoughtfully, he tugged at the lobe of his ear. "As soon as it's daylight we'll take off. I'll probably fly up and down the river first to see if we can locate them. If we don't see any sign of them, I'll notify Tom Fowler by radio to see if he can get some government help to look for them. Then I think maybe I'll go up the river by canoe. There is a possibility that we could see them from the ground when we couldn't locate them from the air."

"You're going to have a language problem in trying to find out what happened," she said, "and in trying to get the Indians to help. Have you thought of that?"

He picked up a pencil from the table and began fidgeting with it nervously. He did not speak for a minute or two.

"Hmmm," he murmured, shaking his head. "I really hadn't thought about that. The man who brought the message to us speaks a little English. I suppose I could use him as an interpreter, if I can't find anyone else who can do a better job."

"He doesn't speak English very well," she continued. "If you try to work with him, you'll have a severe handicap right from the start."

Danny agreed. "Do you have an idea, Kay?"

"It would probably cost you a little time, but I was wondering if we ought to go to Guatemala City first. Tom could be a big help in dealing with the people."

Danny frowned thoughtfully. "He would, at that. But I hate to think of wasting the time. My first reaction is to get out to Castillo as quickly as I can. But maybe it would be best to get Tom."

"I'm sure it would. It wouldn't take more than a few hours if you notified Tom by radio so he could be at the airport waiting for us. The kids and I could stay with Phyllis, and Tom could come back with you." She paused for a time. "Besides, I hate to think of being here at Cielo alone with the triplets under circumstances like these."

He considered her suggestion briefly. "In the long run, it might save time." He reached across the table and took her hand in his. "And I agree with you about the kids. I think it would be better to have them in Guatemala City rather than here at Cielo waiting for word about their parents."

Danny and Kay knelt in the kitchen for a long time that night and prayed for Jerry and Rosalita Davis and their children. At last they went to bed, but not to sleep. They lay there, staring up at the ceiling. An hour or so before daylight, they got up and began to get ready to make the trip to Guatemala City. When breakfast was ready, Danny went into the boys' bedroom and woke them while Kay got DeeDee out of bed. Doug and Del stirred, rubbing their eyes sleepily in response to Danny's call.

"What's up?" Doug demanded.

Danny went over and sat down beside him on his narrow bed. "We're going to Guatemala City."

"We are?" Del echoed, suddenly sitting upright in bed. "You aren't kidding, are you? You aren't giving us a line?"

The missionary pilot shook his head. "No, I'm not kidding. I'm giving it to you straight. We're going to Guatemala City just as soon as you guys and DeeDee can get ready."

The boys bounded out of bed and began to dress excitedly.

"We're going to get to fly to Guatemala City," Del exclaimed. "How about that?"

Danny said nothing about the accident until all three children were dressed and in the kitchen. Kay turned toward the stove and pretended to be stirring something. That was the only way she could keep them from seeing the tears in her eyes.

Doug was the first to notice that something was wrong. The smile faded from his face and the lights in his eyes died away.

"What's the matter, Danny?" he asked curiously. "Is Kay going to have to go back to Minnesota right away or something?"

"Maybe." He swallowed the lump in his throat. "But that's not the most important thing right now." He took a long, deep breath. "Last night we had an Indian runner from Castillo come to the house."

Fear widened DeeDee's eyes. "Castillo?" she repeated. "That's where Mom and Dad are, isn't it?"

Danny nodded. "There's been an accident there, and the chief wants me to come right away."

"An accident?" DeeDee echoed. "Did something happen to Mom and Dad?"

Danny did not answer her immediately.

"If there was an accident in Castillo," Doug said, "why are we going to Guatemala City? Tell me that."

"We need an interpreter for one thing. And for

another, we thought it would be better for you and Kay to be there than here in Cielo while I'm gone."

Del's face blanched. "DeeDee's right. Something has happened to Mom and Dad, right?"

"We don't know for sure."

Quietly Danny told them everything the Indian had said. The youngsters did not cry. The hurt was too deep for that. Instead, they sat there, staring numbly at one another.

"Tom Fowler and I will do everything we can to locate them."

Kay wiped her tears away and came to the table, forcing a bright smile to her face.

"We'd better get started eating. We have a long day ahead of us."

Mechanically the triplets tried to do as they were told, but they couldn't eat much. DeeDee, especially, only toyed with her food. Kay sat down beside her and put an arm around her shoulders. Only then did the tears come to the girl's eyes. They escaped her eyelashes and trickled down her cheeks, but she made no sound.

After breakfast Danny had a short time of Bible reading and special prayer for the triplets' parents. When they finished, he got to his feet.

"You kids get your clothes together, and I'll go wake our Indian friend," he said. "By the time he's had breakfast and you get your gear down to the plane, it should be light enough for us to take off."

The Indian ate hurriedly while Danny was putting gas in the airplane and warming the engines. When the first gray wisps of dawn began to drive the darkness away, they got into the plane and taxied to the end of the runway.

Although he was as impatient to get into the air as he had ever been in his life, Danny waited until he could see plainly before taking off. Once they were airborne, he called Tom Fowler on the plane radio. There was no answer. Kay turned to him, concern clouding her eyes.

"What are you going to do now?" she asked.

He flipped on the transmitter again. "I'll call the airport and have them get Tom on the phone," he said. "They can tell him to turn on his receiver, that I have an important message for him. That ought to get him."

In a matter of minutes the missionary pilot had his co-worker on the radio and asked him to be at the airport, ready to leave.

"Have you notified the authorities, Danny? Over."

"Negative. Repeat. Negative. I thought I'd leave that to you. I didn't know exactly what the procedure would be. Over."

No answer.

Danny repeated his statement. "Do you read me, Tom? Over."

"I read you. I'll take care of it right away. They'll probably want to send in a search plane and an investigator. Over."

"I'm bringing Kay and the kids to stay with Phyllis while you and I go to Castillo. Over."

"Good idea. I'll see you at the airport in about forty minutes. Over."

"Roger. Over and out."

Danny switched off the radio.

For several minutes no one in the airplane spoke. Finally Doug Davis touched Kay on the shoulder. She turned and saw the anguish gleaming in his young eyes.

"Do you think Mom and Dad are–are still alive?" he demanded.

Kay did not answer him. She could not.

"Do you?" His voice rose. "Do you, Kay?"

* * *

Danny landed the plane at Guatemala City and rolled to a stop near the passenger terminal. Tom Fowler and his wife were waiting for them. As soon as the triplets got out, Tom went to the cabin door on Danny's side.

"Ready to leave?"

"As soon as we top off the tanks," he said. "I want to be sure we don't run low on fuel. There's no knowing how much flying we'll be called on to do once we get there."

Danny taxied over to the gas pump and an attendant came out and filled the tanks. In a matter of minutes the missionary plane was in the air once more, winging over the lush, green jungle in the direction of Castillo.

Danny looked over at his partner. "Tell me something, Tom," he began. "You've been out here a long time and know a lot about this country. What are the chances that Mr. and Mrs. Davis are still alive?"

Tom Fowler shook his head. "I wish I had the answer to that question. I've been asking myself about that ever since you contacted me this morning. Jerry Davis is a cautious man, and he knows these rivers almost as well as the Indians do. I can't think of anyone who'd have a better chance of surviving them than he would."

The pilot glanced quickly at him, but Tom continued. "I've been trying to make myself believe that he and Rosalita are stranded somewhere, but, Danny, the Indians in that area are the best rivermen in the whole country. I'm very much afraid they wouldn't have sent for you unless they felt that Jerry and Rosalita are dead."

A little piece of Danny's heart seemed to die within him. "That's what I've been afraid of."

It was a long while before either of them spoke again. There was danger in the jungles. It was the sort of thing a missionary and his family always lived with. He tried to pretend that it didn't exist, that living in Cielo or Castillo was no different than living in a village of the same size in the States or Canada, but he knew better. It was the sort of thing that was always present. He could put it out of his mind, but he could never entirely forget it.

Tom Fowler, too, seemed wrapped in his thoughts. He hunched in the far corner of the cabin and closed his eyes, but Danny knew well enough that he wasn't asleep.

Whatever was done, the pilot told himself, it would have to be done quickly. If the Davis couple was still alive, they would have to find them as soon as possible. They could be badly injured and in need of medical attention and food.

There was a prayer on Danny's lips as he checked their location on the map and corrected their heading by two degrees. In spite of the tension that was building irresistibly within him, he flew with precision. Carelessness now could cause him to get into trouble and would only compound the situation.

In less than an hour they set down on the landing strip near the village. A government plane was already there.

Still the people came out to meet them, silent and unsmiling. Tom got out and spoke to them in their own language.

"Greetings."

The chief stepped forward in all of his dignity and regal bearing.

"Greetings."

"We have come to talk about the accident." There was no polite conversation first – no friendly talk that was so much a part of the peoples' culture. But this time Tom would be excused. There were situations that were too serious to waste time on the accepted way of doing things.

"Sí," the chief acknowledged. He had recognized the airplane even before it landed and knew why it was coming back to his village. "Right away I send two canoe loads of men. Up and down the river they go. They look close but no find anything."

"I see the government men are here."

"Sí." He nodded his head. "Sí, the government men from Guatemala come. They want to look around for the man and his wife, but nobody come back yet."

Tom questioned, "Did the government plane fly over the section of the river where the accident happened?" he asked.

The chief shook his head.

Danny got to his feet and spoke for the first time. "I think that's the first thing we'd better do," he said, "in case Jerry and Rosalita were able to make it ashore."

"I'm positive the Indians have already covered every foot of the river, Danny. It's the first thing they would do."

"Just the same, I'd like to have a look, if you don't care."

Tom Fowler relayed the information to the Indian chief and asked him if he'd go along.

"Sí." He spoke gravely. "I go."

They went back to the plane and, with the chief in the front seat, Danny flew along the swift-running river at an altitude of fifty or sixty feet. He throttled the twin-engine aircraft to a speed slow enough so they could make out every tree and clump of brush along the riverbank.

The murky brown water, almost at flood stage

with recent upriver rains, churned angrily around the broad bend that lay below the slow-moving plane. A heavy log bounced sluggishly over a short stretch of rapids and rifled out into smooth water with only a thin dark gray strip of bark visible.

Danny followed the river to the village of Pieto and beyond, to the Indian camp a few miles upstream. From the moment they passed the little settlement, his passengers stiffened in watchfulness. Shading their eyes with their hands they peered intently at the river below. Danny's own heart was beating even faster. In a few minutes they would have a good idea about whether the missionary couple and their guide had been able to escape the treacherous river or not. It wouldn't be long until they would know whether the triplets still had their parents or whether they were orphaned. Danny's lips did not move, but he was praying earnestly with every breath.

Minutes passed, but there was no sign of anything that could even remotely be considered worthy of investigation. There was the swirling muddy water that lapped within inches of the trees that lined either bank, the tangled screen of vines and brush and vegetation that would have made walking virtually impossible. That meant the passengers in the canoe would have been forced by circumstances to remain where they were if they succeeded in getting ashore. There was little hope that they would be back in the jungle in an attempt to make their way to Pieto.

Danny noted the great, long-legged birds that stood so majestically along the water's edge, their needle-sharp bills poised to strike at any fish coming within reach. And there was a large tapir that moved gracefully down to the river to drink.

But that was all. There was no sign that man had ever set foot on the riverbanks, let alone being there now. There were no paths or clearings, no break in the thick cover of green.

The chilling thought struck at the very center of his bones. If Jerry and Rosalita managed to get ashore, it would be comparatively easy to locate them. Even if they were injured, they would surely be able to make some sort of sign to indicate where they were – to do something to show that they were alive.

At the Indian camp Danny climbed and banked to come around.

"Did you see anything, Tom?" he asked.

"Not a thing." The missionary questioned the chief. "I see nothing."

The ice in Danny's stomach continued to grow, but their answers were no more than he expected.

For almost an hour he flew up and down the river, first near one bank and then the other, flying as low and as slowly as he could in safety. But the answer was always the same. There was no sign of the missing missionary couple or any indication that they could have gotten ashore safely. It was as though they had dropped out of sight, suddenly, and without a trace.

"I think we might as well quit now, Danny," Tom Fowler said. "I don't think there's any use in flying anymore."

With great reluctance, Danny turned back. Never had his heart been heavier. "They must be gone, Tom." His voice was dull and lifeless. "There's little chance that they were able to survive. If they had, there'd be some sign of them down there."

There was a brief silence. Danny reached over and switched on the radio. "We'd better get in touch with Kay and Phyllis."

CHAPTER 8

TRIPLETS' DILEMMA

Back at the village, Danny and Tom talked with the government investigator.

"We have no new information other than what you gave us when you called this morning, Señor Fowler," he said in clipped English. "One of the Indians tells us that he and others from Castillo and Pieto covered that stretch of the river four or five times, but found nothing. There doesn't seem to be any question but that they all are dead."

Danny and Tom nodded. It didn't seem real, standing in the blazing afternoon sun and talking about the two missing missionaries and their guide as casually as though they were as many pieces of equipment. He wanted to shout to his companions that these were real people they were talking about – people with children who had lost their parents.

Even as such thoughts came, Danny realized that they

weren't just. Tom and the government representatives were as concerned as he was. They were only trying to do their jobs as efficiently as possible. The investigation had to be made and a report filed. That was the law.

Soon the government agent finished talking with them, excused himself, and went back to his plane. In a few minutes he was airborne and disappeared in the direction of Guatemala City. Only then did the Indian man address himself to Danny and Tom.

"You knew him?" he asked. "The one who die?"

"Sí," Tom answered. "We knew him very well. He was a very good friend of ours."

The Indian breathed deeply. There was deep emotion in his voice. "He was a good man, that one. He had a love for our people in his heart."

"Sí. He loved your people very much. That was the reason he and his wife left their home back in America and came down here to live."

The silence was taut.

"I am one of those in fishing camp," he went on at last. "I am one of those he was on his way to see when the canoe turned over. He was coming to speak to us again of this One called Jesus."

For the first time in all the years Tom Fowler had been serving as a missionary in Central America, he saw tears standing in an Indian's eyes.

The dark-skinned man swallowed hard. He continued to talk, but it was difficult for him to do so. "Is there anyone now who can tell me of Jesus?" he asked seriously.

"Sí." There was tenderness in Tom's voice. "I can tell you of Jesus, who died on the cross to save you from sin."

The Indian's face lit up. "You speak of Him?" he asked. "You speak of Him now?"

There on the edge of the landing strip with some of the villagers watching and listening, Tom Fowler pointed the Indian man to Christ. He used no pressure. In fact, he only explained. He did not ask him to make a decision. Such was the nature of the Indian people that they had to make up their minds about Christ without any urging from the outside if it was to be a lasting thing – if it was to be genuine from the start. It was too easy for them to agree to something without understanding it, if they liked the one who happened to be talking to them. Still, though there was no invitation, the Indian wanted to kneel and give his heart to Christ.

Danny felt his own eyes fill with tears. Jerry and Rosalita Davis had not only devoted their entire lives to presenting Christ to the lost, their deaths also had led a soul to the Savior.

Danny and Tom flew back to Guatemala City that afternoon to report their sad news. The triplets listened in silence as the two men related that they had found nothing. Kay tightened her grip about DeeDee's shoulders and turned her head away. Only with great effort was Phyllis Fowler able to keep the tears from her eyes.

"Do you think there's any chance that they'll be found alive?"

Sorrowfully, Danny shook his head. "That's what we thought when we flew over the area. But it's no use. We made half a dozen trips up and down the river with the plane and the Indians covered that stretch of river in dugouts a dozen times. There's no possible chance that we both missed them."

Doug looked at his brother and sister thoughtfully. His young mind was in turmoil, yet it was clear that there was one overshadowing question. He turned his ashen face to the missionary pilot. "What's going to happen to us now?" he asked, his voice breaking.

Kay answered him, "You don't have to worry about that, Doug," she said. "You're going to be well taken care of. That's one thing we'll all promise you."

He said no more, but her answer did nothing to ease the uncertainty in his dark eyes. He slumped in the chair and scared with unseeing eyes across the room. Del was in a chair nearby. He, too, was silent. Only DeeDee cried; she leaned her head against Kay and sobbed quietly.

After a time Danny and Tom went out on the veranda to talk.

"I've gone through a number of rough periods in my life," Danny said, "but I believe this is worse than any of them."

"I feel the same way. I think the knowledge that the kids are going to be alone from here on out is the worst situation."

"Whatever happens, it'll be mighty hard on the kids."

"You can say that again," Tom Fowler replied.

There was a brief silence.

"What *is* going to happen to them, Tom? Do they have any relatives to take care of them?"

Tom took a pen from his pocket and held it for a time. "Rosalita's sister lives somewhere in Texas," he said at last. "She's the only relative I've ever heard either Jerry or Rosalita mention. I think her last name was Roper or something like that."

"Has anyone notified her?"

"I called the mission office in New York. I'm sure Dr. Kroeger will get in touch with her before he takes a plane down here."

"Is he coming soon?"

"He'll be here tomorrow morning, I think. He said that he would be coming at once and would let us know what flight he'd be on."

Danny crossed the room slowly. "Is Rosalita's sister a Christian?" he asked.

"I couldn't say. Rosalita heard from her regularly, and I think they were quite close if that means anything."

Danny waited for the clock inside to finish striking. "I suppose it's no concern of mine." He came back and sat down. "But I can't help wondering what sort of a home they'll be placed in. They're good kids, but they're high-spirited and daring. They're going to have to have some solid Christian training and a firm hand, or they might not grow up to be what they should be, or what Jerry and Rosalita would have wanted them to be."

Tom replied thoughtfully, "I think you're right about that."

Tom checked his messages, and in a moment, he said, "Dr. Kroeger will be in on the eight o'clock plane in the morning."

"I'm glad of that. It will be good to get his counsel and guidance in these matters."

The next morning Tom and Danny drove to the airport to meet the mission superintendent. They got caught in a minor traffic jam and were late getting to the airport. When they reached the terminal building, Dr. Kroeger was already there waiting for them. He came hurrying over as soon as he saw them.

"Oh, there you are!" he exclaimed, shaking hands with them. "Tell me, is there any more news about the Davises?"

Tom shook his head.

"We haven't had any good news," he replied. "Danny and I were up the river to Pieto and the fishing camp yesterday, but we couldn't find any sign of them. It seems apparent that they both drowned."

Dr. Kroeger's florid face grew even more serious. "I've been afraid of that."

They went over to the baggage counter and waited for the mission executive's suitcase to come off the plane. While they were standing there, Danny gave him a quick rundown of what had taken place. The older man asked a few questions and finally turned to the subject of the triplets.

"How are the kids taking it?" he asked.

"I don't believe they realize what's actually happened yet," Danny said. "Oh, we've told them that their parents are dead, and they talk about it some, but it doesn't seem to be a reality yet. They're sort of in a daze."

Tom backed out of the parking space and turned into the street.

"We've all been wondering about the triplets," Tom said, concern edging his voice. "Did you get in touch with Rosalita's sister about the accident and the children?"

The superintendent nodded. "I called her as soon as I got the message."

"Did she say anything about the kids?"

"Yes, that was the first thing she asked about. She wanted to know if they were with their parents when the accident happened and how they are taking things."

They pulled up before the house and stopped.

"I'll want to send a message to her and her husband this afternoon." He got wearily out of the car and waited for the younger men. "Undoubtedly there will be some important matters to take care of. I'd like to have her get in touch with us." He paused. "How's the telephone service from here, Tom?"

"Not very good. Sometimes I think it's a little faster than mail delivery and other times I'm sure it isn't."

At the front door Dr. Kroeger stopped. "I don't know whether this would be possible or not, but I've been thinking that I ought to suggest that Mrs. Roper come down here herself. She might want to check her sister's personal belongings rather than leaving that to strangers. Then, too, we've got to find out about the triplets and what's going to happen to them."

Tom spoke quickly. "They can stay here with us as long as is necessary. They wouldn't be any problem at all."

The mission superintendent managed a brief smile. "I'm sure they'd be welcome with you and Phyllis," he said. "And I know Jerry and Rosalita would appreciate it. But from the way Mrs. Roper talked, she's going to be taking them back to Texas with her."

The three of them went into the house, had a belated breakfast, and talked over plans for the balance of the day.

"Do you have anything special in mind, Dr. Kroeger?" Tom asked. "Is there anything you would like to see about today?"

The superintendent paused momentarily. "I've been doing a great deal of thinking about this village of–of–"

"Castillo?"

"That's right. I've been thinking about this village of Castillo where the accident happened. Could you take me there, Danny?"

"Certainly. We can go this afternoon if you'd like."

Dr. Kroeger paused. "I don't think I can go today. There are some other matters that I have to take care of first. How about tomorrow?"

"That suits me fine. I'll go back to the airport this afternoon and check over the plane and get it filled with gas so it's ready to go."

That afternoon Dr. Kroeger sent a message to Mrs. Roper and made some calls.

The triplets roamed solemnly about the house or sat very straight and quiet on the living room chairs. It was almost as though they were beyond feeling. Danny tried to talk with them, but they only answered him in as few words as possible and fell silent again.

Kay was the only one who seemed able to get through to them. She took them into one of the bedrooms and had a time of Bible reading and prayer with them. Later in the afternoon, after the sun had started down and it wasn't quite so warm, she took them for a walk. They were gone for more than an hour, and when they came back, they were more relaxed than they had been since word reached them of the accident.

The following morning Danny took Dr. Kroeger and Tom Fowler and flew up the river to the village of Castillo. He circled and flew back at treetop height and just above stalling speed. The mission superintendent was solemn as they nosed into the landing strip.

"I can see now why you've been so positive that Jerry and Rosalita aren't alive. They couldn't possibly be anywhere along the river and not be seen."

"That's what we figured," Danny said. "If they had been missed by the Indians, we'd surely have seen them from the air."

The lines about Dr. Kroeger's eyes deepened. "I wonder if God doesn't have a special blessing in heaven for those who have given their lives in spreading the gospel?" He spoke quietly, as though he was talking to himself rather than to his companions.

When the plane landed and came to a stop, the narrow runway was lined with Indians. Danny glanced quickly at Tom. "Looks as though we've got a reception committee this morning," Danny said.

"I think they recognized the plane when we flew over."

At that moment a stalwart Indian, whom Danny recognized instantly as the chief, stepped forward and spoke in serious tones to Tom. The missionary responded in the Indian's language. For two or three minutes they talked with one another. Finally Tom turned to the two men who were with him.

"The chief says that his people are still sorrowing over the terrible thing that happened to our friends," he translated. "He says they have continued to look for the bodies since the accident, but they have been unable to find them. He says they are all sorry about not finding the bodies."

"Tell him we are very grateful for their concern and their kindness," Dr. Kroeger answered.

They talked again. Once more Tom turned to the men with him to interpret what the chief had said. "He says that most of the white men who have come here in the past have only come because they wanted to take advantage of his people. But he says that Mr.

and Mrs. Davis showed by their lives that they loved the Indians. And in the short time they lived with them, his people grew to love them."

"Tell them that it was the Lord Jesus Christ in the lives of Mr. and Mrs. Davis that made the difference. Tell him they came out to Guatemala just to tell his people that Jesus died to save them from sin."

"He says he knows that. He listened to Jerry when he spoke to them. He says that his people have been honored to have the white couple come to stay with them and that he and his council would like to ask that somebody else like them be sent to live in Castillo. He said they will build a house for them and make them a canoe and see that they have good food to eat."

There were tears in the mission superintendent's eyes. He turned to Danny and spoke quietly.

"How can we tell them that the Christian young men and women of America are so concerned about having a soft life that we have no one to send to them? No one at all!"

CHAPTER 9

TEMPORARY SOLUTION

That night Dr. Kroeger, Tom, and Danny sat in the living room of the missionary home until after midnight talking about the Davis triplets.

"I feel terribly sorry for them. They're at an age when they need their parents very badly," Danny said. "And now they've lost both of them."

Dr. Kroeger nodded. "It's the children who suffer the most in a situation like this," he said.

"I can't understand why we haven't had any further word from their aunt and uncle telling us when they're going to come after the triplets. I thought they'd get in contact with us long before this."

The mission superintendent got to his feet, crossed the room, and stood before the large window. It was a moment or two before he turned and spoke. "I didn't say anything about this at the time because I had so many other things on my mind, but Mrs.

Roper might not be in any condition to travel. She was pretty broken up when I talked with her. I wouldn't be surprised if her husband had to put her in the hospital for a few days."

Danny nodded. "I can understand that. It must have been a real shock for her to get a phone call that her sister and brother-in-law were both dead."

Dr. Kroeger came back and sat down. "But we still have to decide what is best to do with the children," he said.

"I thought Mrs. Roper was going to come after them," Tom put in.

"So did I. When I talked with her, she seemed to think that was the only solution, but we can hardly take the children to her and leave them unless she says she wants them. And we should be leaving here and going back to the States as soon as possible."

There was a long silence before Tom spoke again. "The triplets are welcome to stay with Phyllis and me until Mrs. Roper is able to come after them if you think that's best."

Thoughtfully, the mission superintendent tugged at the lobe of his ear. "If she doesn't come after them right away – or at least let us know when she's coming after them, I think we ought to take them back to the States with us," Dr. Kroeger answered, "regardless of where they are going to be living permanently."

Danny picked up a pen and held it. He was so concerned with his thoughts he scarcely realized what he was doing. "The triplets probably know Kay as well as they know any other woman aside from their aunt, who might not be in a position to take them for a little while. Wouldn't it be better if they were to go home with us and stay until something permanent can be arranged for them?"

Dr. Kroeger studied the matter briefly. "That's something I hadn't thought about. I'm sure they would feel better if they were with someone they know. I believe that would help to make the days a little easier for them."

Tom Fowler nodded his agreement. "We'd love to keep them with us here. Don't get me wrong about that. But I've seen them with Kay. They've taken to her in a great way." He paused. "She was telling Phyllis how heartbroken she was after the two youngsters you had taken in went somewhere else. Do you think it would be fair to her to ask them to stay with you now, Danny, and run the risk of that happening again?"

Danny spoke up quickly. "We can't have personal feelings in a thing like this. I know that Kay would be the first to think of the kids."

The mission superintendent looked at his watch. "It's getting late. I think we'd better turn in." He got to his feet. "The chances are that none of this will work out anyway. I'm sure Mr. and Mrs. Roper are going to insist on taking the triplets."

Danny nodded. "I was just thinking that myself. We'll probably hear from them before we're ready to leave Guatemala City."

"I hope we do," Tom said. "If they don't come after the kids themselves, the best thing would be for you to take them with you and let them off at their aunt's ranch in Texas on the way home."

Dr. Kroeger was almost at his bedroom door before he turned back. "I don't know why we didn't think of that before, Danny. We've got to get Jerry and Rosalita's personal belongings from Cielo. I suppose you ought to fly out there tomorrow morning and pick up as much as you think you can haul. Then we'll be ready for you to take the kids north if we get word from Mrs. Roper that she would like to have us bring the triplets back to the States."

The following morning Danny was getting ready to go to the airport and fly to Cielo when Tom got a call for Dr. Kroeger. Tom went to the mission superintendent's bedroom door and called him.

"You're wanted on the phone, Dr. Kroeger." Excitement edged his voice. "I think it's the call you've been waiting for."

The mission superintendent took the phone and talked for several minutes. Danny and Tom remained where they were standing, silently listening. At last Dr. Kroeger put the phone down.

"It was Mrs. Roper," he said.

"What did she say about the triplets?" Danny wanted to know. "Is she going to come after them, or does she want us to bring them to the States?"

Dr. Kroeger spoke hesitantly. "To tell you the truth,

I don't really know. When I mentioned the kids, she started crying so hard and began to get so much Spanish mixed with her English that I couldn't tell what she had to say about them. I thought I would wait a little while and call back."

Tears came to Kay's eyes when Danny told her what had happened.

"And," he continued, "from what I understand, she doesn't know Christ as her Savior, so that makes it all doubly hard for her."

"We'll have to remember to pray for her."

Danny and Kay went out to the airport, filled the mission plane with gas, and took off for Cielo.

"It isn't going to be easy to go through Jerry and Rosalita's things and pack them," Kay said hesitantly. "I've been dreading this job ever since I learned that we were going to have to do it."

Danny nodded. "I know it isn't going to be easy," he said, "but it's one of those things that has to be done. There's just no one else to do it."

When they reached the isolated little settlement, they learned that the Indians had been waiting expectantly for them for the past several days. One of the older men came forward to act as spokesman.

"You will come back to stay with us?" he asked. As he spoke, hope kindled in his dark eyes.

Danny shook his head. "No, we have to get back to work in the States," he explained.

"But we need you here."

"I know you need a missionary," Danny went on, struggling for words. "But God has called us to work back there. Besides, my wife gets sick here. The weather is too hot for her."

There was a brief silence. Hurt flamed in the man's eyes. Danny wasn't sure whether he understood English well enough to know what he had said about Kay.

"Will there be anyone to come and tell us about Jesus?" he asked. "Will there be anyone to read God's Word to us and tell us what His Book says we are to do and how we are to live?"

"We are praying that God will have someone to send to work here in Cielo."

Although many of the Indians did not understand much English, it was apparent to them by the look on Danny's face that he had turned down their request. Their faces reflected their sharp disappointment.

Kay choked back a tear and stepped into the little house where the Davis family had lived. "What are we going to take, Danny?" she asked. "Will they want the furniture?"

The youthful missionary shook his head. "I don't think so. Let's leave the furniture and the tools and that sort of thing. The people here can make use of them in case no other missionaries are sent in. Dr. Kroeger thought we should just take personal belongings that would be of some use to the kids or have some sentimental value."

The Indians helped them pack the clothes and books that belonged to the Davis family and carried them to the aircraft. Kay managed to control herself until they were airborne. Once they were out of sight of the people, however, she broke down and sobbed. Danny reached over and laid a hand on her arm reassuringly.

They got back to Guatemala City that afternoon. Dr. Kroeger and Tom Fowler came out to the airport and picked them up.

"Have you heard any more from the triplets' aunt, Dr. Kroeger?" Danny asked.

The older man nodded. "Her husband called a short time ago."

Kay broke in quickly. "Are they going to take the children?"

"Yes, but he wanted to know if you could take them home with you now. He said he and his wife could come to Fairview in a few weeks as soon as she is able to travel."

"We could take them by Texas on the way home," Danny said, "if that would be any better for them."

"That's what I told Mr. Roper, but he feels that his wife needs a little time to get used to the idea before she takes on the responsibility of three more children."

"I see."

"Of course, I couldn't answer for you, but I told him I'd explain the situation to you and Kay, and you would get in touch with him tonight."

Danny glanced at his wife seriously. "What do you think?" he asked.

"Of course we'll take them." There was no hesitation. "How could we turn them down?"

When they reached the Fowler home, the triplets were waiting for Danny and Kay in the living room. Danny smiled warmly when he saw them.

'Well," he said, speaking as carelessly as he could under the circumstances. "We got your stuff. Even your baseball gloves."

"Thanks." Doug cleared his throat. There was laughter in his eyes. "Can we talk to you for a couple of minutes?"

"Sure." Danny went over and sat down. "What's on your mind?"

Doug hesitated, looking first at Danny, then at the other adults who were present, and back at Danny again. "Could–could we talk in your room?"

Questions gleamed in the young pilot's eyes. "Sure, I guess so."

He and Kay followed the triplets into the bedroom and closed the door. There was a brief silence. At last DeeDee spoke in guarded tones.

"We heard Dr. Kroeger and Mr. Fowler talking about–about what's going to happen to us." The girl struggled to hold back her tears.

"Yes?" There was sympathy and understanding in Kay's voice.

"They were talking about sending us to live with Aunt Carmen and Uncle Clarence," she continued.

"They're your closest relatives," Kay explained. "It's only natural that you would want to go and live with them."

The girl's voice rose. "That's just it!" she exclaimed firmly. "We don't want to go and live with them!"

Del turned to Danny. "That's right," he said. "When Mom and Dad and all of us were home on furlough they didn't even come to see us or ask us to their ranch or anything. And when we did go to see them, they treated us as though we weren't even welcome – especially Dad. We just don't want to go and live with them."

Danny waited quietly until Del was able to speak again.

"We–we want to come and live with you."

Kay gasped in surprise.

A tear trickled down DeeDee's cheek. "Don't you want us?"

"Of course we want you." Kay went over to her and enveloped her tenderly in her arms. "You'll never know how much we'd like to have you come to live with us and be our family. But it isn't up to us to decide. Your aunt and uncle can claim you, DeeDee. And because they are your relatives, they have a legal right to you."

Doug's face twisted into a dark scowl. "Don't we have anything to say about it?" he demanded. "We're not like a car or a watch or a piece of property. We ought to have some rights. We ought to be able to decide where we want to stay and where we don't."

Danny answered thoughtfully. "Yes, you have some rights. This is something the courts are very careful to consider. They will want to see that you are raised in the best home possible."

DeeDee stared at him appealingly. "Well, the best thing would be for us to live with you. That's for sure."

"I'm afraid it's not that simple. In making a decision about where you should live, the judge will give a great deal of weight to the fact that your mother's sister wants you. In fact, if their home is an average home, the judge will feel that you would be cared for better by living with them than you would anywhere else."

"But it isn't an average home," Doug protested. "They aren't even Christians."

Danny looked sympathetically at Doug. "I'm afraid the judge won't give much consideration to that as long as they are good, moral people," Danny replied.

"You–you mean we'll *have* to go there to live whether we want to or not?"

"You'll have to do as the judge says."

Kay squeezed DeeDee's small shoulders reassuringly. "We'll be praying that the Lord's will may be done," she said. "And, after all, that's what is best for you, whether it is what we would like or not."

The girl looked up, her dark eyes wide and luminous. "And we're going to be praying that God will let us live with you," she retorted in a firm voice.

Danny spoke quietly. "Perhaps the Lord wants

you to live with your aunt so you can witness to her and her family. Have you thought about that?"

The triplets did not reply.

That night when Danny and Kay were alone once more, they talked about the triplets and the new development.

"It did thrill me to have the kids want to live with us, Kay."

She smiled. "Me, too. But I'm sure the judge will send them to Texas to make their home with Rosalita's sister and her husband."

Danny went over and sat down in a chair. "I didn't know what to say when Dr. Kroeger suggested that we take the kids for a while," he continued.

"I can't see how you could hesitate. The triplets have just had a terrible shock. They need to be with someone they know and have confidence in – for a little while, anyway."

"I wasn't thinking about myself or the kids. I was thinking about you. We had agreed that we weren't going to take any more youngsters into our home because it was too hard on you when we had to give them up. Remember?"

She spoke seriously. "Yes, I remember. And I'm terribly ashamed of myself. I don't see how I could ever have been so selfish as to say a thing like that, Danny."

He nodded. "But it is hard when they have to go."

"I know that, but if we can help them by giving love and understanding and a Christian example, then we're accomplishing a real service for the Lord whether we have heartbreak after they leave us or not."

Danny smiled.

"You were so upset when Kent and Jill left, I didn't think I'd ever hear you say a thing like that again."

"I didn't think you would, either. But this afternoon the Lord gave me victory over it. After Dr. Kroeger asked us about taking the triplets for a while, I realized how selfish I've been. I asked God's forgiveness and for strength and courage to give up the triplets or any other youngsters He might send us."

CHAPTER 10

HOME TO THE STATES

Danny refueled the airplane and checked it out carefully for the return trip to Minnesota, and shortly after dawn the following morning they took off. When they arrived at the airport in Fairview, Danny phoned Pastor Reeves and asked him to come out and pick them up. After introducing the triplets, they loaded their luggage into the pastor's car and headed for town. On the way Danny asked about Jim Morgan.

"How's he doing?"

"Fine. Real fine," the minister said.

"That character only sent us a couple messages all the time we were gone."

The minister laughed. "Well, you know, studies, senior activities, baseball, and a girl don't exactly leave a guy very much time for writing."

Danny asked about how he was doing on the baseball diamond and learned that he had had a sensational season. He had won every game he pitched and batted a surprising .384.

"As well as any of the others did."

"I sure wish I could have been here to see some of those games. They must have been thrilling."

"They certainly were."

The triplets got out of the car at the Orlis house and looked around. Doug turned to Danny at last and spoke in all seriousness.

"I think we're going to like living here with you."

"We sure hope you do," Danny said. "Both Kay and I are very happy that Aunt Carmen agreed to let you stay with us for a few weeks."

"I wasn't talking about staying with you for a couple of weeks." There was a tone of confidence in the boy's young voice. "I'm talking about living here, period!"

* * *

Jim Morgan had baseball practice that afternoon and was late leaving school. He started walking home another way, but at the last minute turned up Danny and Kay's street. He started by the house when it suddenly registered with him that the shades were up, and the door was open.

Danny and Kay were back!

Whirling, he dashed for the house, calling out as he ran. "Danny! Kay!"

Kay came into the living room from the kitchen, a small kettle in her hands.

"Jim!"

He whooped with delight and swept her into his arms. "It's good to see you!"

"It's good to see you, too."

Jim was so excited he was laughing and talking at the same time. "When'd you get back?"

"We haven't been here very long. We just got in a couple of hours ago. We–"

A bedroom door opened, and a slight, black-haired boy appeared, curiosity gleaming in his dark eyes.

Jim stared at him. For the moment he was unable to speak.

"Oh, Jim, I'd like to have you meet–" Kay studied the boy questioningly. "I'd like to have you meet D-Douglas."

The boy laughed.

"Or is it Delbert?"

"Which one do you think I am, Kay?"

She studied his face carefully and threw her hands in the air in a gesture of helplessness. "I don't know. I give up."

"Come on. Don't spoil all the fun. Why don't you take a guess."

Kay laughed. "That wouldn't do me any good. All I know for sure is that you aren't DeeDee."

Jim, who had been listening intently to the interchange, turned to Kay. "What's with all this guessing?" he asked. "What's going on?"

"You remember that I wrote you about the Davis triplets, don't you?"

"Oh, sure. This guy must be one of the boys. Am I right?"

"As right as you'll ever be," Del said. "I'm Delbert, but everybody calls me Del."

"Are you sure you're Del?"

The boy snickered. "If I'm not, I ought to be him. That's the name everybody calls me – unless they're all fouled up and think I'm Doug or something."

Still laughing at the way he had confused Kay, Del went outside. Jim turned to Kay and spoke in low tones. "I didn't know they were coming home with you and Danny."

"Neither did we." She lowered her voice. "But their aunt and uncle in Texas can't take them for several weeks so they're going to live here with us for a while."

The corners of Jim's mouth lifted into a wry grin. "That's great. He's a clever little character. I'll have to say that for him."

"All three of them are. And they look so much alike you can't tell them apart."

Jim went over to a living room chair and sat down.

"It was sure tough for them to lose their parents that way."

The two of them talked for several minutes. Then Kay excused herself and went back to the kitchen. Her eyes filled with tears. It was so hard for the triplets to have lost their parents. And it was going to be even harder for them to go all the way to Texas and live with relatives they didn't like and who probably didn't like them.

Danny had been down to the post office to pick up their mail. As soon as he returned home, he and Jim went to the study.

"I've sure missed you, Danny," the boy said. "It seems as though you've been gone for a year."

"It seemed like a long time to me, too, especially with the sort of a job we had to do."

Jim nodded. For a minute or so, neither spoke. Finally Danny broke the silence.

"Pastor Reeves tells me that you've been doing a terrific job of pitching for Fairview High this spring."

Jim grinned. "We haven't done so bad. In fact, it's been pretty good. We've won all our games so far, and we've played the toughest in this part of the state."

"That's what he said. In fact, he told me you have only allowed two or three runs per game."

"Like I said, it's been a good season," Jim said modestly, "but we've had a lot of luck too. Luck and mighty good support from the field."

"I sure wish I could have been here to see some of your games."

* * *

That night at the supper table Jim got acquainted with DeeDee, Doug, and Del Davis. He liked all three of them immediately. There was a clean, refreshing joy about them that showed through, in spite of their grief for their parents. And their Christian faith was so apparent, so firm and honest.

DeeDee asked Jim about school in Fairview, but the boys weren't so interested in classes. They wanted to know about the baseball team.

"Danny says you're a pitcher," Del said with admiration in his voice. "Have you won any games this year?"

"A few." He smiled in spite of himself.

"Danny says you've won every game," Doug blurted loyally.

"We haven't won them all yet. We've still got the toughest teams to play."

The boys inched their chairs closer to him.

"You know," Doug went on, "I like to pitch too, but I haven't had a chance to do much of it."

"That doesn't make any difference. You've still got a lot of time to play baseball. Why when I was your age, I don't think I'd even had a glove on."

"I've never even been able to learn how to throw a curve."

"I'll tell you what I'll do. Saturday morning when we get the work done around here, we'll go over to the vacant lot, and I'll show you how to throw a curve. Okay?"

The boy's eyes widened. "You aren't kidding, are you?"

"Why would I kid about a thing like that? I'll teach you to throw a curve. There isn't anything hard about it. And if you want to learn, I can show you how to throw some other pitches too."

"Oh, wow!"

"How about me?" Del demanded.

"I'll teach you both if you want to learn."

Doug's young face clouded briefly, and he glanced at his brother. "Oh, don't waste your time with him. He can't pitch."

DeeDee broke in suddenly. "I don't know why you're so interested in an old baseball. I want to go through the school sometime. I'd like to see the schoolrooms and the–the labs or whatever you call them – the rooms where you do special things. I've never been in a real schoolhouse."

Jim grinned at her. He liked the boys, but already there was a special place in his heart for this little girl.

"Sure, I'll take you there if you want to go. But I'm warning you right now. You'd better not linger, or they'll think you're a student and pile some work on you. You're lucky not to have to go to school."

DeeDee's forehead wrinkled, and her eyebrows lifted. "What do you mean, we don't have to go to school? We sure do."

"You aren't going now, I mean."

"We are too going to school now." Indignation colored her voice. "We've got homeschool lessons to work on. And that's even harder than going to a regular school. At least that's what Mom used to say."

Both Doug and Del began to motion to her frantically.

"What's the matter with you? We *do* have lessons to work."

Danny's grin broadened. He alone caught the meaning of the frantic motioning. "Oh, do you? Well now, that's interesting. I suppose you've got them in your suitcases, haven't you? So Kay could get you started on them again the first thing in the morning."

Del exploded. "See, DeeDee! That's what you get for opening your big mouth. We wouldn't have had to do them for a while if you'd kept still. But no! You've got to spill everything you know!"

Danny continued, looking from one to the other teasingly. "I think that was right thoughtful of you, DeeDee. If you hadn't spilled the information about the homeschool courses, you might have been beaten out of the fun of working them while you're here."

Kay broke in. "Danny, don't tease them that way. You know I've been talking about getting them started on their lessons in a day or two."

Del and Doug Davis both scowled.

"Aw! I thought we were going to get out of something."

"So did I. It just about ruined my supper to have those lessons brought up; I can tell you that much."

CHAPTER 11

JIM'S IMPORTANT GAME

Jim was scheduled to pitch against nearby Riverton in one of the last and most important baseball games of the season. Doug and Del had been haunting the practice field every afternoon since they arrived in Fairview, and now that a real game was approaching, they were so excited they could scarcely wait.

"Are you really going to pitch tomorrow afternoon, Jim?"

His triplet brother spoke up scornfully. "Of course, he's going to pitch tomorrow, stupid. He's been practicing all week."

Doug acted as though he hadn't even heard him. "I know, but this is a real game! That's cool!"

Jim laughed. "I'm going to be starting the Riverton game tomorrow, but that's all I can tell you. I might get knocked out of the box in the first inning."

Del spoke up loyally. "You won't get knocked out

of the game," he retorted. "Not the way you pitch. You'll probably get a shutout."

Jim laughed again. "Right now, I'd settle for a one-run win."

Just then Danny came into the room. "Well, how do you feel tonight, Jim?"

He shrugged his shoulders. "Okay, I guess. Why?"

"I was talking with a couple of the guys uptown this afternoon. They said you're going to have a tough go tomorrow. Riverton's got some real sluggers."

"You can say that again. I think the game's going to decide the conference championship – at least, that's the way it looks."

"According to the news, Fairview's slated to get beat."

Del spoke up quickly. "Beat? Why, if Jim pitches the way he did yesterday afternoon in practice, he'll have 'em all handcuffed."

Jim laughed. "I'm glad I've got at least one fan."

The following afternoon Danny and Kay took the triplets to the park for the Riverton game. It was a sunny spring afternoon and half an hour before game time, the stands were packed with people. DeeDee looked at Kay.

"Do such big crowds always come to ball games here?"

Kay shook her head. "Not always. But this game is special. If Fairview wins, we'll be the conference champions."

In a few minutes the players came out and began to warm up. Jim wasn't with the rest of the squad. He and one of the catchers were in front of the dugout near the third-base line. He started throwing effortlessly and not too hard, as though he was playing catch.

When DeeDee saw him, she squealed with delight. "Kay, there's Jim!"

At last everyone stood, and the Fairview high school band played the national anthem. When they finished, the game began.

The Riverton batter stepped into the box, and Jim rifled the first pitch. It was waist-high and caught the outside corner, a blistering fast ball.

"Strike one!"

Jim took the ball from the catcher, held it momentarily, and rubbed it between his hands. The stands were roaring, but it was almost as though he didn't hear them at all. He was tense, but not because of the crowd or the Riverton nine. He was always tense when he pitched.

His curve broke nicely just above the knees for strike two. The batter's swing was late and half a foot too high. The fans were yelling for a strikeout, but the young pitcher threw a ball, high and outside.

With the count of two and one, the batter dribbled a little grounder along the third-base line. He streaked for first, but the leisurely throw caught him by a full two strides for the first out.

The next batter ran the count to three and two before he lined a drive to the second baseman, who caught it without moving a step.

The third batter struck out on three sizzling fast balls that left him blinking, to retire the side.

Fairview managed to get a runner on first because of an error. The runner advanced to second on a sacrifice, only to be caught in a sparkling double play that retired the side.

In the third inning Riverton rapped the first hit of the game with two down. The hit seemed to shake Jim. He threw three straight balls before settling down to strike out the last batter without allowing a run.

In the bottom of the sixth, Fairview's hitters exploded with a three-run rally that knocked the Riverton starting pitcher from the box and threatened the relief pitcher.

But in the top of the seventh, Riverton came clawing back to score two runs before Jim snaked up a glistering grounder that looked as though it was a certain base hit and fired it home to catch the runner sliding for the plate.

That seemed to take the fire from the Riverton team. The last two innings Jim handled the batters easily. At the same time, Fairview scored another run to give a little added insurance. And the game was over.

DeeDee turned to Kay and squealed her delight. "Jim did it!" she cried. "He did it! He did it!"

Doug turned scornfully to her. "DeeDee, pipe down! Everybody's watching you."

Kay was the one who answered him. "That doesn't make any difference. A lot of people from town get so excited about the games that they yell their heads off."

Del spoke up. "If the Indians at Cielo could hear everybody now, they'd think Americans are crazy, for sure."

When they got home from the game, Danny saw there was a message from the triplets' Aunt Carmen. Danny opened it and read it thoughtfully. Doug moved closer to him, eyeing him with great interest.

"What'd she say?"

"She's feeling better now," Danny said. "She says they still want you kids and are going to come for you before very long."

Del broke into the conversation quickly. "Danny, did you ever write and tell her that we're not going to Texas to that old ranch with her?"

Danny shook his head. "She has a legal right to you."

The boy was still not willing to accept it. "I don't see why we can't have something to say about that." His expression changed. "Danny, they aren't even Christians. We don't want to live with people like that."

"We've been concerned about that, Del," the missionary pilot admitted.

Kay, who had come into the room in time to hear the last of the conversation, spoke up. "Maybe God is placing you there so they'll have a chance to see the Lord Jesus in your lives." She paused significantly. "You know your mom and dad prayed for the Ropers for many years that they would accept Christ as their Savior. Now you have a chance to help answer your mother's prayers."

The kids grew serious.

"When you look at it that way," Doug said slowly, "it makes a lot of difference."

"It sure does," Del said softly.

THE
DANNY ORLIS SERIES

The Danny Orlis series, by Bernard Palmer, delivers a blend of adventure, mystery, and suspense through various settings—from the Canadian wilderness to Guatemalan jungles. Danny Orlis, an adept outdoorsman, skilled athlete, and committed Christian, employs his quick thinking, calm bravery, and biblical solutions to confront everyday problems and hair-raising dangers. Early stories focus on Danny navigating school life, sports, and outdoor challenges, while in later books, Danny and his wife Kay provide wisdom and guidance to youngsters facing lifelike situations and challenges. Having sold over two million copies, this series has made Palmer a renowned author in Christian youth literature. Palmer is also the author of the Felicia Cartright series and various other series for Christian youth.

AVAILABLE FROM WWW.ANEKOPRESS.COM

9 798888 936040 7